I Came Erect with the Chill Breeze Starting Tears from My Eyes,

my feet against cold stone in the small square. A white naked woman was running, and the chiaroscuro of that held moment captured weapon flare and the five figures leaping in pursuit black uniformed, and my own body plummeting through space to strike one man to the stinging gravel, time slowly shedding its reluctance, and above all the dreadful fact that I had been here before—that the naked fleeing woman was me and that I had to prevent myself from getting killed if I died in the process.

There was another hiss of weapon fire. I saw an arm coming, caught the heavy fabric and the limb beneath it, pivoted, let the body parabola across me. I leaped high, slammed my foot into a peering face, felt cartilage give.

Lost and anguished, I seized the skcined matrix which trapped me. The gently whispering mechanism of already thwarted death fell in its curved trajectory toward my earlier self at the moment when, with my last strength, I ruptured Time's pattern and took myself into its blackness.

Books by Damien Broderick

The Dreaming Dragons
The Judas Mandala

Published by TIMESCAPE BOOKS

Most Timescape Books are available at special quantity discounts for bulk purchases for sales promotions, premiums or fund raising. Special books or book excerpts can also be created to fit specific needs.

For details write or telephone the office of the Vice President of Special Markets, Pocket Books, 1230 Avenue of the Americas, New York, New York 10020. (212) 245-6400, ext. 1760.

DAMIEN BRODERICK

THE JUDAS MANDALA

A TIMESCAPE BOOK
PUBLISHED BY POCKET BOOKS NEW YORK

This novel is a work of fiction. Names, characters, places and incidents are either the product of the author's imagination or are used fictitiously. Any resemblance to actual events or locales or persons, living or dead, is entirely coincidental.

Another *Original* publication of TIMESCAPE BOOKS

The excerpts on pages 9 and 91 are reprinted from *Come to Me, My Melancholy Baby*, copyright © 1975 by Kate Jennings. Published by Outback Press, Melbourne, Australia. Used by permission of the author.

This novel was completed with the assistance of a Senior Fellowship from the Literature Board of the Australia Council.

A Timescape Book published by
POCKET BOOKS, a Simon & Schuster division of
GULF & WESTERN CORPORATION
1230 Avenue of the Americas, New York, N.Y. 10020

Copyright © 1982 by Damien Broderick

All rights reserved, including the right to reproduce
this book or portions thereof in any form whatsoever.
For information address Timescape Books, 1230
Avenue of the Americas, New York, N.Y. 10020

ISBN: 0-671-45032-8

First Timescape Books printing October, 1982

10 9 8 7 6 5 4 3 2 1

POCKET and colophon are trademarks of Simon & Schuster.

Use of the trademark TIMESCAPE is by exclusive license from Gregory Benford, the trademark owner.

Printed in the U.S.A.

Joanna Russ
for her rage
the sinews of her text

Kate Jennings
utopian anger
made new this book

CONTENTS

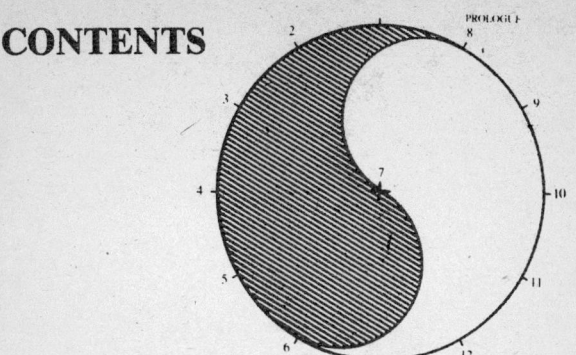

Prologue—A.D. 1999	13
I YIN	15
one—A.D. 6031	17
two—A.D. 1999	30
three	43
four	52
five	65
six	80
II INTERFACE	91
seven—A.D. 6036	93
III YANG	105
eight—A.D. 6039	107
nine	118
ten	135
eleven	149
twelve	159
thirteen	168
Epilogue—A.D. 1966	179

I am waiting for rain
I am waiting for it to rain
I want blood
scalps that made me into
                      a marriageable item a woman
                      who needs a man a transgressor
                      of the moral authority of
                      male supremacy a prison is
                      one twenty years back time
machine, I need nobody but a sicilian revenge,
no triumph.

                                      —Kate Jennings

THE JUDAS MANDALA

PROLOGUE

A.D. 1999

Because the courts permitted me to see my daughter on the first Monday of every month, including leap years, there was at least one compensation for being out of work much of the time. (Thus, my recipe for saying yes to life.) So while everyone else toiled I took the ferry across smooth dark water to the tiny sandstone terraces of Balmain, a snug inner-city gold mine where even the streaky old soap factories (bane of the allergic: invisible gusts of itchy soot) were being scrubbed out and refitted as condominiums.

Once the suburb had been a home for poets and ruffians, and before that the honest working class, whose rampant tasteless ravages had by now been all but expunged. Narrow, overwhelming native gardens soared from tiny plots in front of the terraces. These days the place was too expensive for poets, and the ruffians all spoke Pascal and their lawyers knew to a nicety the lyrics of judicial enchantment.

In all truth, I was in fair spirits. The afternoon promised to be a bitch, mad-dog mutual assured destruction at Central Utility, but that was later. I pushed it away. The day was a delight. Up through the fragrant drying leaves of European trees meant for endless sifting rain the morning sky was hot blue yet pale: the heat in it was not Pro Hart's electric enamel but a kind of shivery end-of-summer immanence, February in Sydney.

I went through Birchgrove park smiling, springy on my toes despite heavy clogs, and even found myself whistling until I realized with a burst of self-reproof that the park sound system was lilting out wimpy Donovan songettes, sticky with adolescent nostalgia and the dying falls of the misunderstood jongleur and scads of sea gulls. Perhaps there had been more sea gulls around thirty-five years ago.

Megan turned from a complicated game with two other little girls and saw me coming up the slope from the sports oval. Shrieking with pleasure, she leapt to her feet, bolted for me, skidded, turned back to excuse herself politely. With some gravity and circumstance her companions allowed her to depart, immediately dividing between them her stock of imaginary play objects. Like a bright yellow bird she darted away again, shot down the grass incline into my arms, and up into the air, the hot transparent air.

"Good girl?"

"Mmm." Suddenly she was shy, pushing her fat pink cheek into my shirt. I went with it, stood her on her feet and took her hand, walked back the way she'd come, up the path toward her school. They knew I was coming and without doubt had me under scrutiny on their monitors, but Spouse Access regulations insisted that I check through the formalities.

Our years put together come to thirty, Donovan told the magpies, almost getting it right. I grimaced horribly at Megan, causing her to laugh helplessly, and whistled along with the awful thing. It could have been worse. It could have been Vivaldi. I might then have broken a tooth clenching my face up, if it had been Vivaldi, plangenting away through the misery and love of a late summer morning as I went to check my daughter out of kindergarten for a few hours of the last remaining truth in my life.

I

YIN

But once I think of an imperfect God, I can begin to imagine a Being greater than ourselves, who nonetheless shares his instinctive logic with us: We as men seek to grow, so He seeks to grow; even as we each have a conception of being—my conception of being, my idea of how we should live, may triumph over yours, or yours over mine—so, in parallel, this God may be engaged in a similar war in the universe with other gods. We may even be the embodiment, the partial expression of his vision. If we fail, He fails too. He is imperfect in the way we are imperfect. He is not always as brave or extraordinary or as graceful as He might care to be. . . .

In capsule: There are times when He has to exploit us; there are times when we have to exploit Him; there are times when He has to drive us beyond our own natural depth because He needs us—those of us, at least, who are working for Him:

We have yet to talk of the Devil. . . .

—NORMAN MAILER

ONE
A.D. 6031

Afloat on a dark hush of air, Sriyanie dreams of dancing.

The gracious moving figures of her dream are vivid, defined, precise:

Taiko gongs. Wind instruments play at Oibuki, pursuing independently their single melody. Each musician tones to the next beat, the following unison, gravely departs again to his own clarity, her own autonomy.

Sriyanie sees this clearly and her ears ring as the Gagaku orchestra brings *jo* to conclusion. With the other dancers she comes forward from the green room . . .

. . . yet she is distinct from them also, at once part of the dream and detached, spectator and creator, her dreaming self the stage.

All through the child's sleeping flesh wafts a breath of subtle particles, responsive to every pulse of her central nervous system. Sensitive as flowers to the sun's warmth, guardian machines inhale that fragrance, cherish her.

Do they know she dreams of dancing? Not precisely. Tropic to the contours and gradients of her sleeping mood, they discern the flow of her burgeoning, the chemistry and alchemy of her pubescent mind.

Her dream has approached lucidity: she suspects that she is asleep. The watchful machines detect her disquiet.

Attaining this state of consciousness is an elementary discipline of the Third Level, and the child, the young woman, is at the verge of passage to Fourth Level. But Sriyanie has not intended lucidity. It troubles her.

The dream, though, is beautiful.

Under a pale green sky, many children watch the Bugaku dance in awed delight. They whisper to one another. Several hold hands. The youngest stir with a certain restlessness.

Upon the great platform is a damask-carpeted stage, and the black and red of the platform's perimeter gleam against the grass of the meadow. The dancers move to a largo pace, then quicken their steps as the second movement, *ha,* is begun.

Joyfully, Sriyanie sees herself dance: the gorgeous Heian costumes—red, purple, and gold, the bright flowers in her hair, the flashing shifts of hue as the dancers disclose the hidden inner sleeves of their gowns.

Sriyanie is a bird, adrift. She knows ("she" "knows") that this is Warawa-mai, the children's Bugaku, a Left-dance, elegant and slow—her departure, in truth, from Third Level. She dances to a melody older than machines, older at any rate than any machine she has ever known, and its Ichikotsuchô mode is alien to the musical canon of her people, for it is based in a tetrachord; yet she has lived now with Karyôbin, the bird, for many months, and the archaic Nihonese music is an intimate caress across five thousand years.

Somehow that immediacy of its patterned beauty alarms her. The orchestration of her sleeping brain peaks and trembles; sadness and loss suffuse the images of grace.

Elsewhere, awake, her Friend is informed of the child's grief and gets sighing to her feet, strangely moved by her little girl's readiness to leave childhood behind. Engineered hormones have retarded Sriyanie's physical development, freeing the child's mind for spectacular growth; she has been prepubescent for close to thirty years. Now mind and body are ready to take the next elective step into maturity.

Beth speaks without words to the guardian machines, goes out into the night air. Third Level youngsters are not permitted to use the Transit teleportation system. For their Friends, therefore, walking is an obligatory act of praise.

In dream the *kakko* player strikes his side drum. They are in the *kyû* movement, dancing allegretto, the *shô* sounding to its player's breath, the tiny *hichiriki* piping like a soul in agony, like the Kalavinka, the magic bird; in its complex entirety the music drones, it drones exquisitely. The dance is near its end. Gong and drum announce their coda of percussion. The splendid, gentle dance is done; Sriyanie is exhausted and elated, transfigured; the child is asleep and the dance is in the child, is done, is in the past, is the past; the blind dance of Sriyanie's closed eyes stills and she stirs, groaning, waking, the aninertial field holding her weightlessly aloft as she wakes, her mood confused and resentful. Beth is waiting in the dim light and takes Sri to her breast.

She holds the child at arm's length and regards her with loving patience. Sriyanie smiles ruefully, knuckling sleep from her eyes, drops her hands to her lap and gazes at them. "I felt so sad, Ummy. Did I waken you?" Through the foul haze overhead a handful of stars glints.

"I was making colors, sweet," Beth says, touching a loose lock of the child's white hair. "You know I don't mind. Would you like to tell me, or should I withdraw for a little while?"

Sriyanie smiles again, a sudden radiance. She puts her arms about her Other and hugs her tightly. "I love you, Beth. Please stay."

For a time they sit in silence. The older woman sinks into receptive meditation, attending to the background murmur of the machines as they cherish the child's integrity, watching her face through half-closed eyes, adding colors to her own private composition.

"I saw the reality of *mujokan*," the girl says at last, slowly. "The—the fleeting impermanence of our lives, of our work. I dreamed the bird dance, and I saw how beautiful it was, and I thought of those silly, lovely Heian people drifting to extinction like falling cherry blossoms, all governed by tact and taste and ritual, and how their freedom was—was isomorphic to the rules of their world, and, I guess, how the Lords restrict us within the bounds of their own possibilities, knowing so infinitely much more than we ever can, weaving their tremendous stupid patterns out between the stars where we can never go, and we're watching from behind the platform while they dance, hardly understanding any of it, and what's worse, even the Lords themselves are contained by limitations of their own, by the cold illusions of their freedom, and Beth, it was so sad."

Her Friend looks at her with grave, tender concern. Beth says eventually: "There's a scene in one of Chikamatsu's plays, *Love Suicides at Sonezaki*, where the lovers begin their final journey. Do you know it, Sri?"

Blinking her tearful eyes, the child shakes her head.

"It goes like this," her Other says, in Old Nihonese:

> "Farewell to this world
> and to the night, farewell.
> We who walk the way to death,
> to what should we be likened?
> To the frost on the road
> to the graveyard
> vanishing with each
> step ahead:
> This dream of a dream
> is sorrowful."

The Friend falls silent, tranquil, the words whispering away into the night. Sriyanie rocks back and forth, cross-legged, taking the ancient lamentation into herself. Then, once more, she begins to grin with suspicion, and sees that Beth is grinning, and her hand steals into her Other's.

"You sly person, Ummy. Well, I suppose an atrocious pun is better than a Zen blow across the head." She adopts a reverent expression and intones the final lines in accord with the phonemic conventions of Mid-English, her special field of study:

" '*Yume no yume koso / aware nare.*' 'This dream of a dream / is aware.' "

She pulls a face and jumps to her feet. Beth rises too and takes a small bow. "I thought you'd like it. But it *is* a useful pun. Awareness replaces sorrow, Sri. I don't mean we should disguise and bind our emotions under a shell of rationalizations. But on a metalevel we know a reality larger than small losses and achievements. We must grieve for a death, but it's foolish to grieve for a life."

THE JUDAS MANDALA

Barefoot, they walk in wet grass, sleeping flowers crinkling beneath their toes. A luminous theorem glows like fire in the sky above the Fifth's arena, its axioms flickering in a gorgeous aurora of transformations. Sriyanie's melancholy is dispelled in the crisp night; her breath puffs on the air; she feels a rush of love for her Friend, her friends, her world. Even the brooding ubiquity of the cyborg Lords, their energies cracking through the world like an invisible, inaudible electric storm, does not blight this new assent.

They come to Beth's privacy, and the domestic machines welcome them with warm odors and warming vibrations. To Sriyanie's astonishment, Beth leads her through a dull red shield to the Transit locus, then faces her for a moment, holding both her hands.

"Let's go see the sunrise on the beach at Suva," Sri's Other suggests buoyantly, and the tiny cues of her body, the minute pressures of her fingers are saying suddenly in an urgent kinesic tongue: *Trust me, open yourself, expect change; little love, trust me.*

"Transit! Am I ready? How wonderful," the girl says dubiously. "I'm hungry, Beth—are you? Shall we have fish?"

Beth nods, and Sriyanie steps forward for the first time into the teleportation locus. The scintillation of Transit discontinuity sings in her body. She expects instantaneous transition to the resort dome at Suva, protected from the befouled environment by its filtration field. She expects to find people stirring to the new day, a tang of freshwater fish on coals, the boom of waves beyond the filter field, the greasy, mother-of-pearl gloss of the poisoned ocean. Instead—nullity. Numb—nowhere—

The child screams, and there is no sound. Her mind plunges, flailing without motion, draining to some nadir of dread that is total inaction. In the no-time before awareness is finally lost she clings to the memory of her Other's hand: *Trust me, little one, trust me.*

Her central field of consciousness, of being, sustains appalling paradox. She dissipates, tenuous as vapor. Simultaneously she undergoes catastrophic implosion, the universe recedes, she suffers ultimate, singular density. Suspended, dispersed, a frail bubble of grotesque mass, her being drones, drones exquisitely, to some august derivative of the cosmic inertial frame.

It is dark, dark, deepest red. What are these forms, limpid, fugitive, a geometry of edges limned in gold and purple, gentle pressures, passing from nowhere to nowhere? She rocks back and forth, slowly, slowly, to booming, delayed echoes. Bright stars reel past sunbursts tasting of gems. Light ebbs in sluggish waves, rolling in pale bands and bands of darkness. Percussions rise and fall, climbing, pounding through bone and nerve as glimmer makes shadows, grow and thrum and dominate her rhythms like the throb of the ocean, like a primordial heartbeat ...

Reality is a soft cage, a comforting restraint of vertical shafts, an irksome debility. She is depleted, miserable; she draws the warmth and the pale glow to herself, encloses it within her, sucking. Brightness regards her. Gratitude surges like a tide. There is Another. She reaches for the warmth, crooning with love, holding to that trust she has almost failed, and recognizes Beth.

Ummy, she says, *Ummy, hold me.*

Sri, her Other tells her, *I love you, love you.*

Painfully, exuberantly, she rebuilds her world. The void is not without form. At one pole she retains herself, at the other her Other. Between them, the pulse of energy elaborates its grid, its field, its intricate, manifold relationships, its matrix. Does she build the world? Does the world disclose itself to her? She sees that both are true. She takes colors from the void and shapes them; they tint the patterns of the void. Many people laugh. Many people speak, disputing. Many people weep. She has invented them all. Beth is with her. She is not Beth. She is like Beth. She is like herself. She likes herself, and Beth, and the universe they have built. She turns, withdraws, broods, grows unhappy with her work. Why must Beth plague her with her presence? Violently, she repulses her Other. She modifies her work, tampers with its shape. She feels pain. She feels joy. She cannot find Beth, and she weeps, tasting salt. She is in the sea, and the salt fills her mouth, her hard teeth snapping against a melancholy of blood.

Ummy, she cries, *hold my hand.*

The world jigs and capers. In the gibbering confusion Beth grips her hand. Strata slide and grind horrendously.

She constructs taxa, and pays the toll, then giggles and groans at her cosmic pun. Expectation swells within her, seethes; she tenses her muscles and fixes her gaze, and grips Beth's hand, and leaps—

They tumble together into sand. Sriyanie hoots, turns her shoulder into the hot white sand of a featureless beach (hot?) and goes heels over head, comes up snorting, and flops to her knees to stare at the crashing white waves in the endless, surging ocean. Beth brushes sand from her own hair and examines small dry shells. Sriyanie runs heavily to the edge of the water and dips her toes into clear, frothy ripples (clear?).

"Wow." She scans out to sea. Tiny white sails dance at the deep horizon. "It's *beautiful*. Where's the pollution gone?" Her face creases; she says in puzzlement, turning, "Hey, Ummy, there was something weird about—"

Dread assails her. She has expected sunrise, but here the sun has been up for hours. Beth sits cross-legged on the sand beside a glowing fire pit which was not there an instant earlier. Silvery fat fish wrapped in large leaves char on the coals. Sampling a glass of some sparkling liquid, Beth holds out the bottle toward her.

"Breakfast'll be ready in a moment, Sri. Come and sit by me."

"Where did the *fire* come from?" she asks shrilly. "Is this a cyborg simulation?" In horror she stares at the pit, knowing that it is not a simulation, knowing that Beth would not have brought her to a simulation.

Her loathing is ghastly in its effect: the fire vanishes.

It is no longer there. It might never have been there.

Beth rises from the unmarked white sand and comes to her as she stands trembling.

"Too fast, pet? But now we have no breakfast. Look." She gestures, and the fish are there again, cooked now and piled on a woven platter. "I made it up, Sri. Then you unmade it. But it's real, Sri. Hang on to that fact. Here—have something to eat." Gingerly she picks up a hot fish and passes it to the girl. "Mm." Beth licks her lips. "Tasty. Try some—you'll like it. Watch the bones."

Sriyanie takes the fish and places it between her teeth. The aroma is superb. She bites the firm white flesh. She cannot bring herself to swallow it, and spits her mouthful onto the sand. She remembers how she and Beth built the world, and the knowledge is too awesome, too large to absorb.

"We made it up?" she says in a small voice. "We made all this up?"

"Well, sort of." At last Beth smiles. "You did most of it. I just helped tidy the edges."

"Where are we, Beth? Beth, am I still asleep?"

"We call it Timestop, pet. Our duration is at right angles to the prime metrodynamic. We've shunted out of Transit, and we can stay here as long as we like before we complete the transition to Suva. It's basically Third Level math, but you won't really appreciate the fine points until Fifth. Sriyanie," she adds, proud and formal, "you've now been initiated into the first of the Great Mysteries. As soon as we get back from Suva you'll be promoted to Fourth Level." Discarding formality, she hugs the girl fiercely. "Now, eat your fish and we'll see what we can dream up to drink with it."

When they have eaten, Sriyanie squats in the sand and retracts her attention. Absently she slows her pounding heart, hushes the thousand anxious voices of her autonomic system. An immense joy sweeps her. Now that Beth's calculated, shocking challenge has been met, her profoundly trained mind sorts and matches what she has learned with what she has known previously.

She discerns gaps in her mathematical model of the universe where she has never noticed them before. The epistemological requirements for this ontology, this radically new foundation for existence, map themselves outward and inward from her painstakingly provisional verities. Immediately, logical bridging transformations generate themselves. Intellectual excitement makes her sweat and shiver. She sees how Timestop is inevitable. And something else is clear: this is an aspect of the universe which the cyborgs have never uncovered.

Aloud she posits quietly, "The Lords don't know about Timestop."

"Cyborg percept-concept-action structures," Beth tells her, in mathematical notation, "are categorically prohibited from this condition. It is a function of purely organic life alone."

"Then we're truly free," the child breathes. "They have limits we do not. Beth, Beth, why didn't you *tell* me?"

"You were not ready," her Other says. She speaks in chomsky, the basic language she shares with Sriyanie and the other Frees: the syntax of her utterance provides its own unassailable conviction. "Besides," she adds, "there are societal restraints as well as epistemological ones. The cyborgs must never learn of Timestop. It's our only retreat from their total surveillance, our minimal advantage. One day, we hope, we shall learn enough about the dynamics of time to make it more than that. For now, the fact that Transit gives us access to another universe, another condition of being, has to remain secret. We've developed techniques for blocking cyborg deep probes, but they can only be implanted during Timestop itself. I'll help you do that shortly. Do you see why I couldn't tell you about it before?"

"Yes, Beth. Thank you," says the girl, and withdraws once more, her thoughts accelerating, the webs of concept and action broadening and growing robust. Above her, the sun moves toward noon in the improbably clear sky. She has put it there. Sweat springs from her skin, trickles in her armpits. The wine is clean and tart on her tongue; she puts down her glass and shades her eyes, glorying in the universe she has hewn with Beth.

"Let me tell you a story," her Other says, turning over and digging her elbows into the sand. "It's a very old tale, one of the oldest we know. Have you heard of Oedipus, the Swollen-Footed King?"

"I don't think so. Greek?"

"One of the mythic figures of the archaic Hellenic culture," Beth says. "His father was King Laius, the Left-sided; his grandfather, Labdakos, the Lame. Laius is banished from his city of Thebes and develops a homosexual bond with the charioteer Chrysippus, his patron's son. In time he regains his throne, marries Jocasta, but refrains from heterosex because an oracle has revealed that her son will kill him. During a fertility rite, though, Laius grows drunk and lustful, and Oedipus is conceived.

"The baby is consigned for execution to a herdsman and staked by his foot to a chilly mountaintop. Before Oedipus can perish from exposure, however, a peasant finds him and rears him in secrecy.

"Years later, the adult Oedipus returns to Thebes in a chariot and meets Laius on his way to the Delphic oracle.

During an argument over right of precedence on the road, Laius causes his son's horse to be slain. In fury, and ignorant of their relationship, the young man kills his father.

"Subsequently the road to Thebes is terrorized by the Sphinx, a monster. To win the widowed Queen's hand, which is the most direct path to political advancement available to him, Oedipus meets the monster in contest. He is riddled: 'What creature goes in the morning on four feet, at noon on two, and in the evening on three?' He answers correctly: 'Man.' In mortification the Sphinx takes her own life."

Sriyanie has been listening with keen interest, playing sand through her fingers. She smiles.

"For many years," Beth says, "Oedipus reigns in Thebes, fathering children by Jocasta, his all-unknown mother. As you can see, the chronology is somewhat strained; the ancient Greeks had no antiaging drugs. Well, at last Thebes is afflicted with plague and famine. An oracle reveals that the cause is royal incest and the parricide which made it possible. Jocasta commits suicide and Oedipus goes mad, tearing out his eyes. He leaves the city once again, attended only by his daughter Antigone, and eventually attains supernatural insight."

Beth falls silent. Sriyanie gazes at the dazzling waves, musing.

"It's lovely, Beth," she says. "Austere and terribly somber. I think I'll suggest it for a Being-Them." She sucks at her lip. "I guess Antigone came back to Thebes and took the throne?"

"No. Oedipus had sons also—it was very rare for women to rule."

"Oh. Then I imagine the rightful heir was driven out and came back eventually to seize the crown."

"Something like that. If I remember properly, Eteocles banished Polynices, who brought back an army, and both the contending brothers were killed. You see something cyclical, then?"

"Beth, it's so rich in resonances I don't know which harmonic to start with. It taps right into the deep structures. But, look, if it's a myth it can't stand by itself. It's just one element in a huge redundant cultural mosaic, and anything I see must be so partial—"

"Naturally. But, Sri, myth is also cellular, holonic. Within the larger context, each part has its own integrity. Tell me what you got."

"Well, right, the basic structure's cyclical, but it's also paradoxical. And there are strong cybernetic features: the road to Thebes is obviously part of a primary information circuit, a model for data flow and decisions, and the Sphinx catapults that up to a metalevel. I mean, roadways are the most blatant symbol any low-mobility culture can use to work out their problems with internal and external dynamics. There's also that beautiful loop where the Urban child is menaced by the Pastoral intermediary, and saved by the Agrarian benefactor, and comes back to master the Town, and ends up transfigured again in the Rural domain."

Beth considers her through a mesh of lashes. "Low-mobility cultures also placed great store by kinship regulations."

"Oh sure," the girl says dismissively. "There's that whole strident incest thing, with Laius symbolically fucking his son, and Oedipus actually fucking his mother, and their town getting the pox. That's only a surface reading, I'm sure—though I daresay the old storytellers did plenty of winking and nudging. What fascinates me is the deep resonance. You know, it's extraordinary: the whole thing's about us and the cyborgs. The dreadful road to high technology. Where it leads, and the way out. Maybe the way out."

"You understood the meaning of the Sphinx's riddle?"

Sriyanie preens. "I've heard of walking sticks. And chariots. Yes, Beth. Man begins as an animal, passes through the bipedal state of hunter-gatherer culture, freeing his hands to use tools, and finally leans so heavily on his technology that it's completely introjected. Actually," she says with surprise, "I guess there's a sense in which that's true of individuals, too: crawling on all fours as babies . . ."

She trails off and immense shock shows in her face. Abruptly she jumps to her feet and runs to the sea, discarding her robe, and splashes wildly in the ebbing tide. Waist deep, she submerges, comes up coughing, light glinting from her pale body. The water lifts her like an aninertial field, tugs her gently toward the long dark line of the horizon. Shrieking in delight, she turns, paddling clumsily, forges to the shore, races in a dog-legged curve of deep footprints back to Beth.

"It's all about me," she gasps, out of breath, flat on her back. "Me and Timestop and that weird thing that happened. Ummy, you *are* sly! It's a myth of the steps in the development of personality."

"Bravo!" applauds Beth. "Don't give me too much credit for ingenuity, though. The old psychologists recognized as much thousands of years ago, as far back as Jean Piaget. Some of them even used it to denominate the principal saccadic stages of individuation: the Oedipus Nexus."

"Yes! Yes!" Sriyanie cries. "So, to incorporate the metalevals lots of the details are apotropaic, conveying the exact opposite of what they actually mean. Old Swollen-Foot begins in the sensorimotor stage—and one limb is crippled! He develops through magic omnipotence, climaxing his journey through the preoperational stage with the ultimate magical act of killing his father. What's the next bit? Why, yes, to attain adult estate he's obliged to deal at the concrete operational level with a riddle—and the riddle, of course, is a rebus for the entire myth, mapping individual onto cultural development. And when he finally passes into the formal operational stage of adulthood, his insight into the kinship crime represented by his incestuous marriage hurls him into mystical consciousness. It's all elided and compressed, but it's all there."

She is fairly bouncing with delight. "Oedipus tears out his eyes *because* they are the organs of guilty perception. And that loops right back to his crime, since a baby's first social transaction is with her mother, through their mutual gaze. And mystical insight requires a new metalevel anyway, going beyond rigorous formal operations into antinomies and paradox. I'm devastated, Beth. How sublimely those old savages captured it all!"

Her drying hair clings to her scalp like pale fronds. Beth musses it and gets to her feet. All trace of their repast is gone. "They weren't really savages, Sri. They were at the very beginning of the path leading to the industrial cities, to the thinking machines. They had no inkling of Timestop, though, I imagine. That had to wait until metrodynamic discontinuity, though some of the scholars disagree with me on that. Why do you think the story is about you?"

THE JUDAS MANDALA

They climb the sand hills, away from the beach. Insects buzz among the flowering grasses, the tropical trees.

"Well, this virtual matrix we're in was built up the same way. I knew you were with me, but I felt omnipotent . . . and lost. Then the phylogenetic codes came snapping in, one by one, and everything sort of . . . crystallized." She stops, perched on one leg, and looks searchingly at her Other. "What would've happened if I'd come through into here on my own? Psychosis?"

"If you'd made it," Beth agrees. "I doubt that you'd have been able to. It's a complicated trick, and only a very stable, imaginative adult mind can originate it. Youngsters entering Fourth Level are guided in. If a child *did* come through without support? It's a horrifying thought. Total solipsism, I suppose. Something like the cyborg Dreamvats, but worse—there'd be *no* constraints. A mad god in a closed universe. We stabilize our generated reality here by consensus, and that includes sophisticated social compulsions as well as the phylogenetic deep structures."

The child shivers. She plucks a ripe fruit from a tree and bites into it. Rich, luscious juice covers her chin.

"You said this is the first of the Great Mysteries," she says thoughtfully. "Ummy, when am I to be initiated into the rest? Or shouldn't I ask?"

Her Other reaches up, takes a fruit from the same tree. "The Second Mystery is greater than the First," she says. She eats the fruit slowly, regarding Sriyanie. Like a mother, then, and like a priest, she lays her hands upon the girl's shoulders.

The world fades back into forms without content, into lines and points of vivid hue. Once more they are suspended in the void. Beth's gaze is warm and bright, tranquil. The bond between them streams with light. Beth's soul opens; her childhood, her growing up in the embrace of her own Friend, her abundant adulthood: her being.

Trembling, the child enters the door.

Sriyanie is Beth, is Beth, is Beth.

TWO

A.D. 1999

After my day at the Taronga Park zoo with Megan, hot but with breezes coming off the water, the animals panting in shadow, the unemployment office was stifling and dismal. Central Utility is not big on finesse: they believe, I suppose, that comfort accelerates moral decline in the jobless. I slouched self-destructively on the hard, cramped bench, trying not to look at the extraordinary young woman who moved deftly beyond the partitioned counter. Commanding my lust, I heedlessly folded and mutilated my function-status sheet. The middle-aged Taiwanese squeezed next to me grumbled unhappily. Relenting, I adopted a more reasonable posture and shoved the tattered form into my belt pouch.

The young woman still refused to catch my eye, and none of the other staff seemed interested.

I uncrossed my legs and let one numb foot clatter heavily on the floor. People scowled. With the exception of several adolescent louts, who reveled in the idea, none of them cared to identify with the category which circumstances had allotted them. I wasn't all that charmed myself.

The young woman had now dealt with two clients who'd come in later than I, and was apparently lining up a third.

I'd abandoned remonstration; it invariably led straight into one of *their* zero-sum routines, and guaranteed a counter-productive outcome. I began to wonder if I were wrong after all. Maybe what looked like a meaningful anomaly was merely a statistical artifact.

"Roche!" Uh-huh—her voice.

Sighing, I ambled to the counter and leaned on it. Grooved with pencil scorings like an ancient school desk, its surface was almost tacky to the touch. With a stiff finger, I nudged my crumpled function-status sheet toward the young woman.

"It is now five weeks," I said fairly loudly, not without rancor, "since I registered the fact of my unemployment with Central Utility."

Her hands (wonderfully pale, considering the summer we'd had) trod a pedantic path down the yellowing keys of the console. Discreetly, beyond my direct view, her information screen cast up the bones of my biography.

"I shall be even more precise. I do not have a job. I am getting hungry. My feet are growing cold at night. I am very unhappy."

The sardonic tone sort of faltered about then. Detached, unmoved, the exquisite woman let a felt-tipped pen stab from one square on the parkinson form to the next.

"You have applied for the three jobs we notified you about last week," she stated, scrutinizing the form. Placing the pen carefully on the counter, she looked hard at me. "None of the prospective employers accepted you for a position."

"That's right. Not even for an interview. I'm delighted," I said, "to find that you can read."

Teeth, very white; nostrils crouching back. "Your attitude has not improved, Ms. Roche."

"We've been having these little chats for over a month now," I said. "I believe our relationship has attained sufficient intimacy for you to call me Maggie."

Her *Weltschmerz* intensified. "Maggie, this department doubts that you are really interested in employment. If your demeanor in this office approximates the way you present yourself for a job, it is not surprising that you cannot find work." The human retina is not designed to read blue-lit computer script upside down on a slanting screen; I quit trying and let my spine unkink. "The department may be forced to recommend the suspension of your Relief credit. You *are* entitled to alimony, you know."

I got up on my toes. My teeth, too, are white and sharp.

"Listen, sister, don't read me your sexist rule book. I am twenty-nine years old, and sound in liver and lights. I have a postgraduate degree. If I decide on prostitution I won't require the judiciary to peddle my snatch for me. I want a job." Two Asian refugees without a word of English between them edged away, feigning interest in polyglot posters.

"I'll tell you something, Maggie." Her voice was neutral. She gazed out a fly-spotted side window. She was pale as frost and showed me her splendid negroid profile of strong cheekbones and soft hard-edged lips. "You have been dismissed from three professional and eight semi-skilled positions. Why do you suppose that is?"

"Why indeed?" I said sweetly. "Perhaps I'm just not lovable." I was finally convinced that her appalling piquancy represented some purpose hardly designed to bring me joy. From the outset she had broken all the rules and then broken the rules governing the permissible exceptions to the rules. She was patently in the wrong place, which made me angry and linear instead of ruminative.

"You are an arrogant bitch," she said in the same dispassionate tone. Astonishingly pale lashes screened the dark-in-bright arc of her gaze. "No matter where you go, you know it all better than anyone else. Inside a fortnight you can be guaranteed to have abused your employer, disrupted your fellow employees, and very probably debauched the entire staff, male and female. You are an insolent, supercilious, insufferable trollop."

This was better than I'd hoped for. Something inside me danced a manic jig. "The rent has been due for three weeks," I said. "I'm still waiting for a goddamn job."

"Have a seat for a moment, Maggie."

"Shit, why not? I think I'll move my bed in here."

I went back gloomily to my paperfax, Professor K. R. Barnes's *The Great Recession*, a barbed, incisive little number with more than a few undertones of déjà vu.

I have only vague memories of the Recession, for all that we're still on the gray, attenuated arse-end of it, but cybernation and "resource management" don't seem to have made much difference to classic scapegoating techniques. I grinned in appalled recognition at Barnes's account of Recession image points. One really is tempted to entertain twenty-year cycles. Dear dead Goebbels, McCarthy, their ever more lackluster disciples. Two decades ago I'd have been one of half a million "dole bludgers," an idiom peculiar to Australia, which pleasingly yokes (1) gorging at the public trough with (2) leeching the bestial earnings of prostitution. We didn't talk about dole bludgers anymore; instead, so my newsfax commentators told me, I was a "relief licker," which invoked instead a coprophagic flavor.

"Roche."

"Yeah."

The young woman slid open a drawer, her hands flashing out of sight and ripping. She conjured forth a torn-edged sheet and lettered carefully on the blank side. "Be at that address at eleven tonight," she told me.

"A trifle late for an interview, isn't it?"

"Do it." She walked away calmly to another cubicle and beckoned one of the migrants. He smiled gingerly and stumped over to her. I jammed the slip of paper in my pouch.

The office door's electronic reflex coped.

My dingy little room was squeezed between a wheezing lavatory and a peeling wall at the top of four flights of rickety stairs. On the top step I slipped off my right clog in accordance with a recent ritual. I battled the key into a long-abused lock, finally lost my temper, and kicked it open with my bare heel.

The rat scampered from the sink across to the crack in the floorboards. I slapped the light on and sent the heavy clog sizzling through the air. The wall shuddered; a few gray hairs lolled as my sly companion skidded to cover. His eyes seemed to glint back at me in stupid derision from the shadowed hole.

I sat down on the bed and took off the other shoe. Apart from a few good graphics, the room was dull with neglect, cluttered with pencil-lined paperfax, hologram snips, unwashed clothes, dead bottles, and a scatter of miscellany. Even now, with the sun tossing its final gold for the day into the sky, the cement walls of the tenement radiated oppressively. I shoved together the last couple of wholemeal crusts and chunks of tepid rat-molested cheese.

Feet clomped up the stairs. I nibbled without enthusiasm. The lavatory flushed, gurgling. I lay back and noticed the envelopes on the floor where they'd been pushed under the door. Must have been stuck in the wrong box by our retarded postman. Headache pulsed over my forehead. I picked up the letters and dropped them on my stomach, one arm across my closed eyes.

The woman's outburst had been too specific, much too personal, too calculated. The procedures of Central Utility, as of any other government instrumentality touching the general public, are not intractable to analysis. They stand in inverse relation to the natural protocols of common sense and ordinary civility. It could scarcely be otherwise, since they are born of an obscene mating of clerical resentment and manipulative policy. Since quite obviously the most efficient, empathic, useful clerk–client dealings are grounded in consistency, the principal rule at Central Utility is that one never sees the same staff officer twice. Even with perfect information retrieval consoles, this permits a stunning degree of mutual incomprehension, temporizing, imputations of bad faith, and the multiplication of misery. Yet the young woman had now interviewed me five times in five weeks. There was nothing accidental about it.

I gained no comfort in recognizing the popular stigmata of paranoia. It *was* that: the loom of events that spun out the image of my life was weaving someone else's pattern. Sister owl, you're too cynical for delusions of persecution. Still . . .

Darkness fell into the sky and a breeze nibbled at the newsfax pasted over the broken pane. It carried off some of the muggy heat. I looked at my watch and found only the white against tan where my watch had been. Cursing, I rolled over and turned on the prehistoric valve radio. Above me the dusty light bulb flickered peremptorily and went out. I sighed, rummaged in my pouch for a bobby pin, and went out down the stairs to twist it into the overloaded fuse box.

THE JUDAS MANDALA

I came back up tired, sickened, and angry at my pigsty life. There arrives a time when viewing the world as *absurdité* is merely and utterly demoralizing. The letters lay on the rumpled blanket. I tore them open, found another overdue notice for power credit, a very polite account from my Attack instructor, and a sharp imperative from my ex-husband's solicitor demanding that I restrict my access visits to once a month.

The old radio crackled static out of its mangled intestines. I thought about Megan, and her absence was a lump in my body. The bewildered face of her father jumped at me. Our marriage had been an incredibly dumb idea. Beneath what James was (for which I had married him) was what he had been born and bred and never gotten over (for which I had broken things in vile furies). He was, in his agonizingly sincere fashion, a true son of the patriarchy. It is hardly my nature to submit: I will love my love and be mother to my child, but I have no fondness for kennels. I lost my child when my husband, with the blessing of the male courts, took his dignity and grief back into a world where I would not and could not follow him. But it was still raw and sour, and it hurt.

I turned the distorted radio down, twisted the letters together, and threw them across the room.

From the corner the rat ran.

I seized a metal-shod clog and hurled it. The gray shape staggered with slow, shocking heaviness, squealed, and lay still with blood running from its snout. After a moment I heaved open the paper-pasted window, picked up the dead rat by the tail, and lobbed it into the dry lank weeds below.

My back arched. The nerves of my arm jumped with shock. The murdered rat had weighed in with the mass of a fair-sized brick.

I ran downstairs into moonlight. The broken rat lay amid smashed bottles and parched grass. I carried it back to my room on spread hands. Its coarse fur was warm. It was impossibly heavy. It was an impossible rat.

A bread knife makes a clumsy scalpel, but the animal opened out like a perfect, expensive mechanism. A pair of blue-membraned cylinders sat in its entrails, wired in a superb confusion of infinitesimal circuits to the major ganglia. A set of golden threads hooked into its spine. I prized open its skull as delicately as I could and considered the fantastic grid of its caged brain.

I tugged out the filaments connecting them with the dead beast's nervous tissue. Jesus, I thought, what *is* this thing? I stopped abruptly, seeking the difference in the room. Beyond my breathing, music played low and without distortion.

A biofacted spy. According to the underground press the CIA had R and D'd them, but no one without a badge had ever seen one. Its transmissions had been screwing up the radio. For a mad moment I thought of James, but then the answer was plain enough.

My hands were trembling. I wrapped the bloody carcass in old newsfax, wiped the cylinders, and set them cautiously to one side of my dressing table. Against all odds the hot water supply was working; I lathered my filthy hands and rinsed the soiled bench. My brain refused to produce cogent linear output. I dried my hands on a blanket, sat down on the creaking bed, and pulled from my pouch the folded slip of paper the Central Utility woman had given me.

In its way it was no less extraordinary than the doctored rat: finely woven paper, yearning to be bound in tooled leather. Perhaps it had been. It suggested cozy private libraries, an era before holograms and microfiches. It was not the stuff of interoffice memos or employment office slips.

The message was simple enough: an address on the edge of the Malcolm Fraser National Park, well north of Sydney, where cybernation magnates and mining industrialists hold court in high-synergy mansions amid hectares of nicely tended timber and flora. It named no names. Presumably I was expected to go to the maids' entrance. Below the address it stipulated 11:00 P.M. sharp.

On the reverse side, in elegant type, was a poem.

Above the poem was a line of curious symbols. Below that, in concave brackets: *JUVENILIA—The First Poems*.

I read the first of the *First Poems*. It was pretty bad.

There comes a time when shock has expended its reserves, exhausted its mandate. Carefully, I refolded the page and put it back into my pouch.

THE JUDAS MANDALA

I felt no impulse to check through my thin sheaf of unpublished verse, less to open the even slimmer *sheet metal* volume. I knew I had not seen that poem since I had destroyed the only copy a decade before, when I'd made a bonfire of all my baby efforts.

In the vague dusty light of my ugly room I hunched, knuckles cracking white and blurred near my face, elbows jammed into the vulnerable flesh between ribs and hips. An old nightmare perspective from that poem's pubescent time suddenly caught me.

—A stalactite, I was hanging outward by my heels from the scabby rind of the tilting earth, its black globe tumbling above me like an idiot's toy from the dark unknown to the unforeseeable dark, tumbling around a glare-yellow star that fell through its own flame.

Cramp brought me out of that. I forced myself to stand up. Dizzy, I grabbed for an internal gyroscope aligned in some more acceptable reality. And what reality does *she* represent? Christ, I thought, what bizarre reality spies on me through the eyes and ears of a wired rat and publishes deluxe editions of my lost childhood scribblings?

I got out my handkerchief then and had a good howl. When that was over I made a cup of coffee. Look, I explained to myself, snorting, even in our depraved goddamn patriarchy there must be *some* rational constraints on watergating. The police had no quarrel with me; writing poetry had not quite attained the status of a felony. Even the celebrated madmen of Security Intelligence could have found no cause for alarm. I was as overtly political as a stale cigarette butt—and so were my parents before me, come to that, considering the time scale suggested by the poem. My own brand of tired nihilism was inoffensive to all but the most evangelical witch-hunter. The feminist underground themselves had no more reason than Security to waste time watching me through an expensive, illegal sensory snoop.

My mood swung from vertigo to manic anger/silliness. I scratched through assorted junk in my pouch and extracted a meager collection of small change. For a moment I gazed dubiously at my moribund credit card, shrugged, and thrust it in my back pocket. The lock jammed itself again with a grating sound as I closed the

THE JUDAS MANDALA

door behind me. I reaffirmed a vow to smack my landlady one in the eye next time she ventured into my path.

The tenement's public phones were in a puce-walled alcove at the foot of the stairs. Old meals and stale piss. I turned my shoulders to the wall as an aged woman with monumentally veined nostrils heaved her bulk up the stairs, grumbling as she came. "None of the poxy things working, dear," she muttered bitterly, squinting at me.

"Ah, well, Mrs. H.," I said, hearty but without conviction, "I guess I'll try my luck anyway."

She vented a cynical, phlegmy snicker without looking back and labored up the groaning steps.

I dawdled until she was out of view. One of the units bore a host of wounds; some rebel youth had vigorously cast off his primal awe of the instruments of tribal communication. The other two phones, though battered, seemed in fair order. The payboxes took either card or coin. I hooked out the wads of paper I jammed into the coin slot when I was flat broke. Each phone yielded a couple of coins. Sorry, Mrs. H. I dropped one back into each of the machines. The screens blued. I checked the directory and keyed the first phone.

"Central Business Register," stated a tired switchgirl. It was the first time I'd ever been grateful that all Commonwealth cybernated departments are operational twenty-four hours a day, three shifts keeping tab on God's Lucky Country.

"Corporation," I requested.

The screen went to direct microprocessor function.

"I wish to register a new company," I said, articulating my consonants.

"Please state your name," the computer displayed in bright, neat, leaping lines, "those of your associates (if any), your credit code, your current address, and the nature of the proposed company."

"Lily Cousland Short," I answered briskly. My landlady would be furious in several days, when the appropriate parkinson forms arrived for her written endorsement. Stuff her. I gave the necessary misinformation and added, "We wish to begin the flower-pressing aspect of our service immediately. We've already been inundated by orders from enthusiastic prospects." I was riffling through the directory and began keying another number on the adjacent phone.

"Thank you, madam," displayed the computer. "Kindly stand by for a brief processing scan."

"Certainly." I nodded. "I'm much obliged."

"Central Utility," said the second screen.

I crouched, presenting the top half of my face to the other camera, and tried to look like a dwarf lady capitalist. "Labor deployment, please."

When the computer logo appeared I supplied the same identification, requesting a status report on a prospective employee named Marguerite Roche, address thus and so, credit code whatnot.

"We have no Company registered as 'Mother's Happy Blossoms and Floral Tributes,'" the computer accused. "Access to privileged data is accordingly denied. No private individual is permitted—"

I said sternly, "The company application is being processed at Central Business Register. Check with them." I bent back to glance at the first screen. It still showed a holding pattern.

A thin fox-featured tenant, skulking on the stairs, jangled coins in what must have been intended as a peremptory manner. "Listen, sweetheart," he began in a whine, "you can't—"

I looked at him coldly. "Police business." The screen buzzed. "Get your arse out of here."

He'd seen me around before and he hesitated. I bared my teeth; his eyes slid away and he scurried out of the alcove into the street. The buzzing was repeated. I turned back to the screen.

"Please clarify your last statement," the microprocessor demanded.

"What? Uh, sorry—I was reading a bedtime tale to my baby daughter."

Unperturbed, the computer cleared the display. "Further information is required concerning details pursuant on potential debenture stock—" The second screen sounded. "Hold," I said. "One moment, please. I must confer with my colleagues."

The other phone wrote: "Employability function-status

on Marguerite Roche, divorced, is available to the personnel officer of your proposed company, Mrs. Short. However, a preliminary scan indicates a total lack of prior flower-pressing expertise on the part of—"

"I'm handling personnel," I assured it. "Screen the data now and mail a fax for later reference." The hard copy would cost the bitch a ten or two, a small deposit of grief that made my lips twitch.

My mirth was brief. Computer script punched down the tiny screen, spelling out a concise curriculum vitae and credit rating. The first phone was yelping for attention. I ignored it. "Cancel that fax order," I said faintly, and blinked at the screen.

Small wonder no employer had got round to granting me an interview.

Under the heading Criminal Record (if any), my data file provided a short, brutally succinct, wholly invented catalogue of convictions for offenses against the state and the person. They characterized the kind of revolting pathological maniac you wouldn't be seen dead with, though the chances were good that you would be. I felt ill. I wanted to run out into the street screaming, "I didn't do it!"

I closed my eyes tight and performed some rapid arithmetic. According to the listed prison terms, I'd started my felonious career at the age of eighteen months. Several terms, even so, had been served concurrently.

Naturally, no personnel officer could be expected to make such a calculation. His own computer's edit parameters would bump me straight off the file long before he got to eyeball the candidates. The information retrieval system *had* been known to make mistakes, but not of that order.

Until now. And that one wasn't all.

The other phone was still bleating. I reached around the dividing sound baffle and cut the call off; it had served its purpose. I stared back at the second ludicrous assertion. Prefixed by an unfamiliar symbol, my credit rating informed those whose need to know let them look at it that I was worth slightly in excess of $100,000. Inflation-stabilized dollars at that: a year's salary, *sans* tax.

The file abruptly faded. The desk girl peered out at me. "Mrs. L. C. Short?" Her tone was sharp.

I tried to focus my mind. "Uh, that's right."

She considered her console telltale and thinned her lips. Her degree of sisterly solidarity seemed marginal at best. No doubt she believed she was winning because she had a job. "There is some question of authorization concerning the inquiry we have just interrupted."

"What time is it?"

Automatically she glanced at her watch. "Nine fifty-two." Her eyes jumped with suspicion. "I must ask you—"

"Don't let it worry you," I told her tiredly. "See, *I'm* smiling." It must have looked like a death's head in rictus. "Have a nice night."

"But—"

I nudged a plastic button blackened by nicotine. Her face dwindled: Alice on the wane. I stretched my cramped shoulders and moaned. Behind me, the scrawny tenant edged toward a phone, telling himself that even weirdo undercover lady cops must be human. I rewarded his faith with a dazzling smile.

Halfway up the stairs I changed my mind. Jesus, I told myself, let's see just how far this thing goes. I shot down to the alcove again, hooking the plastic card out of my back pocket. The man shied. His conscience must have been somewhat on the grubby side.

I dropped the card into a slot and keyed for a non-cybernated Credit Check.

A brisk crew cut appeared. He punched his console, glanced at the telltale, looked up with a quizzical smile. "At this moment, Ms. Roche, your credit stands at exactly seventy-one cents. Minus the charge for this call." It was terrible news. I sagged with relief.

"However," he added, his smile broadening into affable camaraderie, "a stipulative promissory transfer in your favor has been put on notice. It becomes operative at midnight tonight, if your transaction is concluded successfully."

"A hundred thousand dollars," my voice said.

"Correct, ma'am. It will then accrue standard interest unless and until you reinvest the sum."

"Thank you," I said, reaching for the cutoff.

"You're more than welcome. Feel free to call for advice at any time." If I'd waited any longer he'd have invited himself around for a drink.

I went back to my room, turned on the radio, and looked at the fly-speckled light.

"What transaction?" I asked it.

THREE

A ticket to the next station but one got me onto the platform. In fact, my destination was the other side of the harbor, thirty minutes away by fast rail and another twenty by foot, a residential area far too refined to possess facilities for anything but yachts or ground-effect transport.

There's little joy in arguing with electronic exits, and still less in flashing a conciliatory tit at the ticket inspector. I dropped out of the car from the wrong side onto paper-littered stones between tracks. The air was pleasantly mild: it had soothed away my headache. I clambered up the flowered slope edging the line, glad I'd decided not to wear a dress. Late summer jasmine and black-eyed Susan were gray and clear in the moonlight. Beyond a wooden railing at the top, the least distinguished residences of the locality brooded in glum resignation. I started walking.

Halberd-topped spears thrust from the loam in a vast fence guarding the address I had been given. Hectares of grassland, copses of English trees planted generations ago, lofty white eucalypts like lonely sentinels, sculpted settings of native flowers behind the great fence intoxicated my eye and all but hid the large house in their midst. I came to locked arabesqued gates. Huddling beside them was an open gate on a human scale. I put my hands into the back pockets of my jeans and went up an internal road of white sand.

Little by little, the house revealed itself as the most extraordinary structure I had ever seen. The woman at Central Utility had accused me, justly enough, of arrogance. My arrogance leaped up to fuse in admiration and fellowship with the maniac who had yoked together the dynamics of this building.

It was that astonishing, improbable thing: a successful amalgam of idioms mutually alien, forms and motifs pitted one against another across continents and centuries. It was as miraculous a gestalt as Antonio Gaudi's Casa Batlló.

I am a poet by instinct and profession. Poetry does not pay my bills but that is what I *am,* despite the conviction of our time that poetry is a senseless antiquated ornament. I walked incredulous in the moonlight and felt that house burning in my flesh. Great silver-blue blocks of stone, maybe hewn two hundred years earlier by convicts, tumbled upward against gravity on each other's shoulders, to a single slender minaret; adzed red gum grew from sandstock, confronting images of men and beasts fashioned in welded steel; windows of colonial proportion held glass shaped by lead, some glowing, some unlit, promising glories of shattered color in daylight.

I moved on crushed sand in the green odors of grass and tree and felt the hair pricking my scalp. Whoever had dreamed and built this place was well down the road to megalomania, but nevertheless had thrown out a challenge to that nameless reality we have always felt impelled to worship, and the challenge was not unworthy.

A soft night light drew me to a marbled piazza half hidden by lush bougainvillea. An opossum bigger than a fat cat belted down a tree trunk and ran in front of me. My throat contracted. I went unwillingly toward the light.

An arched door swung open as I stepped into the loggia. Clearly, my approach had been noted by a monitor mechanism. Oddly, again, that tension between old and new was not unharmonious. I let my hands drop and went into the house. Behind me, the door quietly closed. I passed through an empty anteroom and stopped.

Darkness velvet, darkness gleaming. The room, as I

entered it, seemed a place of no fixed dimension. Yellow and red, muted, glimmering, echoed from wall to pawfooted chair to ancient tapestries of hunt and hunted. Light, where light was, glowed like burnished brass under oil. A post-Vasarely hologram hung in space above the veined marble of a shadowed fireplace.

The woman stood almost lost in darkness, her hands cupping crystal. No hint now of the distant, efficient clerk with whom I had dealt for five weeks. Nor was she the afternoon's provocative, incisive tactician. Slender in shadow, in the warm old tradition of the room, she was strange and lovely and authentically feminine. I waited.

"Good evening, Ms. Roche," she said, her vivid eyes taking a crescent of brightness from the crystal bulb she held at her lips. "You are seven minutes late."

"Yes, it was silly of me," I said. "I let the chauffeur off for the night."

"Quite so." She smiled. Her head went down, drawing out the last fumes. It was all so absurdly theatrical that I wanted to slap her. She lowered her arm and bent to place the crystal on the table at her hand. "Maggie," then, she cried out. Two strong hands were choking me, gouging my larynx.

My left hand struck up, slammed the assailant's little finger back into agony. Left clog found his shin, slashed toward the bone. I pivoted, dropped low with the man trailing the pain of his trapped finger, then drove the rough edge of my free hand into the side of his neck. He jerked convulsively and left his throat vulnerable. I let go his savaged finger, bunched my left fist, struck his larynx with the extended knuckle of my index finger.

He coughed, an ugly, absurdly deep liquid noise, and collapsed at my feet. I left my legs slightly bent, waited in *Zenkutsudachi* for further attack. I only started sweating at that point. "Shit," I said. "Big deal." I was frightened but beginning to believe they weren't serious about it.

Behind the woman, a man almost concealed by a highbacked leather wing chair turned silently to face me. Tall and spare, in his mid-fifties, he rose laconically to his feet. I had failed to see him earlier because his clothes, his black hair, his deeply tanned face were modifications of the darkness.

"I am impressed," he said dryly. To the woman he said: "Ms. Roche may care for a drink. I must call Dr. Williams to look at poor Teddy." He crouched for a moment at the fellow's side, examined his bleeding leg, touched his throat lightly. He regarded me, then, and bowed his head courteously. "My name is Elfield, ma'am. Permit me to make a suggestion. There is a phone in the next room. I would like you to dial a Credit Check on your account—"

"I know," I said angrily. "You're bloody mad. What transaction?"

He was slightly taken aback. "Consider it a gesture of good faith, Ms. Roche. I would be pleased to discuss the matter further over breakfast. I believe you've never been formally introduced to Ms. N'Zanvy. Sriyanie, could you show the lady to her room?" He inclined his head again. "I must fetch the doctor. Good evening." He was gone.

The fellow on the carpet moaned and threw one leg about. I crossed the room to Sriyanie, still out of breath. "Shall we go to bed?"

Her face, so far as I could judge in the auburn light, was paler than usual. "*Would* you care for a drink?"

"No." The touch of astonishment went some way toward compensating me for my furious bewilderment. "You might like to make one up and leave it for our friend here. His bruises are going all nasty and blue. When we're in bed you can tell me all about it."

"It isn't nice," she said, with a return of composure, "to go about with your teeth clenched."

"It never did Mona Lisa any harm."

She opened the door without once looking at Teddy. I decided she didn't care for the sight of blood. "Why do you presume I will be sleeping with you?"

"I've seen the movie," I explained, following her closely.

She halted, turned. "But what gives you the idea *you* have star billing?"

For a moment, gooseflesh marched up my back.

Where might I earth my anger: in what archetype? In her flesh.

My baffled hostility, my equivocal lust sought outlet. This woman was at once source and object of my passionate confusion. I placed my hands upon her and lacked, in that hour, the perception to find in her response neither fear nor masochistic acquiescence but some complex engagement. My ignorance appalls me.

There came a time of repose. Above us, a chandelier glowed the dull blue-purple of ultraviolet. I thought it was weird and tasteless, a stage set, out of keeping with the glorious folly of the house. The huge low bed was nearly invisible; Sriyanie and I were smudged against an iridescent whiteness of sheets. Shimmering to an inverted radiance, the sheets seemed to float suspended above the floor.

I lay on my side and thought of Alice in Looking-Glass Land. If that nimble child had slipped through a mirror into a world of reversed parity, we were in some universe close to the photographic negative. Perhaps their set piece was intended as a metaphor. For what? I put my hand on Sriyanie's stomach. Her smile glimmered like the Cheshire Cat's; she touched the fingers pacing the hollow of her navel.

"Well," she said, "I can see why."

I placed a finger across her mouth. "Let's forget the debauched office girls."

"All right." She offered a contented sound. "Add one to your list."

I sat up and hugged my knees against my breasts, wanting a cigarette. Our bodies were flaw-dappled in the macabre antilight, a manifesto of mortality. Neither of her shoulders showed inoculation reaction pocks. "Sriyanie, let's skip that bullshit. I don't know how or why you've been standing behind that Central Utility counter, but it isn't because you're saving for a new cotton dress."

"Maggie," she began.

"Or a new Bentley."

"No," she agreed quietly. Taking my hand, she drew me down beside her and put her chin on my shoulder. "David and I have been looking for . . . a rather special kind of person. I've been searching for six weeks."

"I'm it?"

"You heard him. I guess you're it." There was a lot more than that to be said, according to the tensions under her skin. She said nothing.

"Well," I said. "Let's hope I didn't mess up your rough friend too much proving it. Or your goddamned snooping rat."

"He was paid to take risks. And I'm sorry about the rat. There were things we had to know."

I ignored her. Maybe, in an abstract sense, we're all minor pieces harried hither and yon in the endless deterministic game generated by eight billion people struggling for existence in an uncaring cosmos. But learning that your paranoid fantasies are true is intolerable. "Elfield," I said, finally putting it together. "David. God on a crutch."

His face had been on *Time* a couple of years before. Head of the Bateson Institute. The R. D. Laing of chip technology or something. No wonder he could get his hands on a biofacted rat. It didn't explain the poem.

I stepped out of bed and foraged in my pouch. I stuck the torn-edged sheet under Sriyanie's nose.

"This went into the furnace ten years ago," I said. "Where did Elfield get it?"

"Don't ask me any more questions," she said, her tone curiously pleading. I wasn't in any mood to listen. She pressed a control at the side of the bed and the shimmering violet light faded out. Warm soft arms wrapped around me. "Let's just go to sleep. I can't tell you any more yet."

Confused and angry, I pulled back and got a cigarette out of my pouch in the pitch-dark. "Sriyanie, there isn't anybody who's even *seen* that poem."

"You showed it to Nigel," she said quietly.

"Jesus, is there anything you bastards don't know? Nigel has been dead for fifteen years. And that doesn't explain why you had the thing printed up like this. Are you running some demented psywar project on the vanity of social misfits?"

Sriyanie rolled away from me and refused to say another word. After a time, her breathing slowed into sleep. I smoked one cigarette after another, in the dark, crushing the butts into the carpet. I brooded on poetry and its risks.

In itself, poetry was a kind of metaphysical hazard. For a utopian anarchist (which is what I was, despite my protective pose of sour nihilism), I'd adopted a curious art. For what could be more hieratic, rank with private enclosures, elitist, than the distilled elixir of poetry?

At the time I entered upon my tertiary education (1988, University of Sydney), the Kuhnian dialectic had swung the needle of fashion in the Literature Department back firmly into the quaint doctrine that Art was a thing unto itself. Prose and poetry of the great must be quaffed with neither aperitif nor coffee, not to mention soup, pudding, brandy, and nicotine. The words on the printed page, that is to say, were the whole feast. My tutors, true children of the prevailing moral climate, urged a virginal innocence, a trembling approach, a long engagement bereft of instruction manuals, and a regular churching. Naturally, the promised joys of intellectual ravishment were generally marred by the equally prevalent frigidity which this procedure encouraged.

I snorted to myself in the dark, half asleep. Sriyanie did not stir. What did she and Elfield know about Nigel? I had been a troublesome child, a burden to my parents and mentors, gotten at by poets before I reached the University. What I saw on the page of a book compelled me, but not to the exclusion of what lay at the top of the ropes of neurons which worked the muscles which directed the pen which preceded the typesetting. As a kid I'd had the good fortune to love Nigel for a short time. Not as a daughter, not as a lover, not as a colleague, not as a student, or not wholly as a student: I'd loved the old turd because he was a poet and a good man, and I'd seen him kicked to death on a greasy footpath, and lost more than one kind of innocence when the cretinous shits who did it turned their attentions on me.

Poetry was personal. It came from real people, anchored in their time and place and passions. Fear and anger and love were never far away. So I had not been taken in by the academy. Context, relation, relevance, texture: text. Perception to conception to that central bond with its thousand strands to concept to percept. Were we joined, flesh and spirit, in some holy synapse of the noosphere? Or did we purchase growth at the price of identity? Was the alteration which art worked on us like syzygy, that presexual mingling of genetic materials enjoyed by simple cellular organisms clever enough to see that cloning is a downhill dive into entropy and ruin? If each of us is enhanced by art, at nobody's spiritual cost, what bounds are we obliged to set before transfiguration enters the void?

Despite his leanness, Dr. David Elfield was not a small man. As he bent over a huge high-protein brunch, I sipped grapefruit juice and let myself merge into the harmony of the rock garden.

Late morning heat drove the air into wavering veils. Gray pebbles seemed to be a rough flatbed of solidified mist under the distorted air. I was reminded inevitably of Ryōan-ji, the most famous of Zen contemplative gardens: motionless rocks in a tide of dry, ancient stones. Sō-ami, its Buddhist designer, would have appreciated the skill with which Elfield's garden had been sown out of Chaos. Which is not to say that he would have been pleased: there was an additional element here, intrusive of Japanese tranquillity, elevating the garden beyond perfect stillness and rest. In the center of the sea of rocks, four living flowers made an explicit affirmation of life and seasons.

Elfield followed my gaze. "'Heaven and earth and I are of the same root,'" he quoted, smiling. Sriyanie made her way carefully across the pebbles, bearing steaming black coffee. There was no counterfeminist passivity in her. She was Elfield's equal. A casual observer might not have noticed.

I recognized the quote. "'The ten thousand things and I are of one substance.' Yes. But this is no Zen garden, David."

"No," he agreed. "This dragon stirs even here. If he must perish, it should be in violence and wrath, not with quiet regret." I failed to understand him for a moment, recalled then that Ryōan-ji is the "place of the dragon's repose."

"The whole world," added Sriyanie's cool voice at my shoulder, "is stinking in its own passivity."

"You amaze me." I waited for them to state their business with me.

"Marguerite," the psychologist said, "it was once my ambition to create a total environment art. Instead, my interests were directed to more inward dynamics. In the process, and to my considerable surprise, I became wealthy enough to build this house." He looked down on the four blooms mirrored by diamonds of water in the alabaster fountain. His fingers dipped the water. "This garden is my favorite place. The Arab poets spoke of such a setting. Its very smallness, they said, is its enchantment. If great gardens circle a house with all the bright botanic riot of Allah's inventiveness, still the little garden is the very wisdom of flowering things."

He lifted his gaze. "As you can see, they were not mistaken, Marguerite."

David Elfield possessed unquestionable force. I felt the strong currents of vitality flooding out from him, girdling the three of us irresistibly. His formal serenity clothed the vibrancy of some great wild creature. With every word he spoke I became more fitful, more unaccountably disquieted.

Elfield was looking raptly at the four blossoms. The rose was a flame of red gold, a glowing fire of joy, a velvet blood-tinted cloud. Tall and lonely, the tulip was a flaming coal unconsumed, an ancient intoxicating wine undrunk. The white fragility of a hyacinth held high its flower like a swan upon unbroken water. And the carnation was an incandescent bubble, a crystal fragment torn from the western sun. Elfield lifted his furrowed, weary face.

"Marguerite," he said, "we wish to offer you the future."

FOUR

I walked back to the table, sloshed coffee into my cup, and fought my anger. David Elfield and Sriyanie N'Zanvy (what the hell kind of name is that?) followed me in silence. Calmly the man let himself into his chair and lit a long brown cigarillo.

"Dr. Elfield," I said, not gently, "your methods are somewhat indirect."

"As they must be."

"I am tired of riddles and charades," I said even more loudly. "In saying that much I am doing you a greater courtesy than you have done me. You've put me through your cryptic hoops for reasons you decline to specify intelligibly. In return I have shared your hospitality. My curiosity can compel me only so far."

Sriyanie's lips quirked.

Flushing, I stood up again. "Even that." I started for the door.

"And where will you go?"

I halted, turned, my voice slightly shrill. "That's my affair."

"True." But Elfield too rose, his hands extended toward me. "It is also my affair, and Sriyanie's."

THE JUDAS MANDALA

"Why should I waste any more of my time?" The money in my credit account was utterly irrelevant.

Elfield laughed with engaging warmth. "You ask for a sign? Come, sit down. I'll endeavor to make matters clear."

I returned to the table and seated myself, anger cooling, my curiosity piqued again by his extraordinary manner. And Sriyanie took my hand across the polished bamboo and smiled.

"You're a splendid anachronism, Marguerite," said the dark man, offering me a cigarillo. "In this appalling era you represent an abundance of vitality and a sensibility for desolation that is truly paradoxical."

We were slipping back again. "If you mean that I'm a woman, a poet, and out of a job, I'll agree with you."

"That's the beginning of what I mean," Elfield admitted. He looked across the sullen gray stones, slain fog where the full sun smote the rock garden, to the radiant blossoms. A fine mist sparkled its lucent rainbow above the cool alabaster and brash sunlight fell back astonished. "Marguerite, words can't easily broach what we are going to show you. The most significant aspects of the universe can be approached only with a kind of shy respect—they do not lend themselves to dissection."

He held up a cautioning hand. I let my mouth close without words.

"As you say, you're a poet without work. That is partly our doing, but I don't apologize for abetting the inevitable. In essence you're a woman badly adjusted to your time. This millennium is drawing to a close in a mood of decay and retreat. All the necessary violence of profound rebellion has been blocked by the violence which maintains the status quo. If your soul is suffocating, Marguerite, its cry won't be heard. Ours is not a time for boldness. It is a time which does not *dare* heed poets."

I knotted my hands on the table. "Even so, you seek out a woman poet for your undefined task?"

"In a time like this," said Sriyanie, "only a poet retains freedom of choice."

"These sentiments are not exactly newly minted," I said. "I want to hear the details of your commission."

Sriyanie pushed back her chair and stood up. With a swift economical movement Elfield gathered together plates and cups and went into the house. Crisp sweat provoked my nostrils. It might have been my own. Certainly, though the sun was hot enough in the suddenly vulnerable enclosure, I was surprised by the damp clinging of my blouse.

"It's futile to explain what must be experienced," said Sriyanie, motioning me into an austere hallway which opened off the rock garden. I followed her into the sudden gloom and cool. "We will give you a sign." Again that strange hint of biblical foreboding. I felt my curiosity gusting to apprehensiveness.

We paused for a moment before a scanning mechanism at the end of the hall. The massive door slid back into the wall. Bright lights came on inside a large white room.

Four deeply padded variable couches were positioned about the room, like a nightmare of dentistry. Projector lenses glittered in the ceiling. Chillingly, in the clinical asepsis which otherwise permeated the place, an array of wooden Sepik River totems and masks presided in primeval solemnity.

Smiling reassuringly, Elfield came in and the heavy door closed again. "Make yourself comfortable on one of the couches." He went to a tray of syringes which sat on top of a complex control unit. Dear God, not the mad scientist and his beautiful companion.

I stayed put, though, holding Sriyanie's gaze.

"We're going to initiate you into the largest enterprise any human being has ever undertaken."

Her enormous calmness took my wind away like a blow to the belly. We had in a moment passed outside the accepted parameters of corporate, sanitized, oppressive sanity. I was hooked. I trusted her.

Sriyanie came and stood beside me. She made minor adjustments to the couch, then sat at its foot.

"Maggie," she said, "thirty years ago the psychedelic pharmaceuticals enjoyed a brief vogue." Her speech was too fast, couched in a peculiar pedantry which only accented her nervousness. "It coincided with technocracy's first spasm of defensiveness. You were only a baby—" She seemed to stumble mentally. Rapidly, she said, "Persecution by the establishment was inevitable, because a psychedelic revolution would have snared the best minds of this failing culture. It would have shattered the status quo completely." The academic detachment of her words was painfully close to ludicrous. "The prevailing ethos in the West would have disintegrated before the more viable energies in its midst and in the East."

"I've been stoned on occasion," I said dryly. "I didn't know it was that apocalyptic."

"Ah, but it is," said Elfield's deep voice, "it is. Potentially so, certainly, if it had spread out unchecked through a culture so utterly alienated from subjective realities."

He grasped my left arm, pushed the sleeve up, held the pressure gun against the artery. A coolness tingled.

"That was a psychedelic?"

"A specific, short-term, highly sophisticated psychelytic," agreed Elfield. "I want you to lie back and go with it. It's quite safe, but rather disconcerting."

Dizziness, suddenly.

I bit into my tongue for words. Futility drained me. It was no product of the drug. I struggled to deal with the matrix of absurdity which was the last twenty-four hours. Pattern eluded my grasp. I was constricted by irresistible pressures. My own personality was one of those impelling forces. I sank amid waves and did not quite suffocate.

"Look," I struggled to say, "I've read Huxley and Watts and Lilly. I know about serotonin and endorphins. There's nothing particularly startling about psychedelics, except that you can go to jail if you're caught. What do you expect to prove?"

Sriyanie sat slightly tense at the end of the couch, swinging one leg. Above me, distorted by his nearness, Elfield exhaled smoke.

"Don't misunderstand us," he said, drawing a stool to the side of the couch. "That injection is merely a convenient instrument. What we're going to demonstrate could perhaps be achieved as easily by fetching you a hefty blow to the head. Of course, that would hurt more."

"Maggie," I heard Sriyanie say, "trust us." My attention plunged into a wasteland of noise.

In that moment of dissociation a shrill whine of webbed light pulsed high and painful in a field which enclosed Sriyanie, Elfield, and me. It had not come into existence at that brief instant; it did not depart when my failing consciousness lost hold of it. Simply, terrifyingly, I knew that it—endured.

Hands smote me into night.

THE JUDAS MANDALA

I was borne up into darkness and fear.

Shadows from childhood stalked me. There was no light at all, no definition. Voices muttered and groaned beyond the ear's threshold, awful antique whispers which shredded my courage.

My hands clung in rictus to the edges of the couch—

—and I knew there was a couch.

Muscles slack with fear jerked into tension. My body fought the horror of paralysis in darkness. I pushed myself up on one elbow, slithering in my own sweat. The skin seemed flayed and open on the palms of my hands.

I hurled my slaughtered body from the couch. Cold wet weft of fabric pressed between my toes and into the soles of my feet an infinite distance below. On bent legs, swaying, I howled within my mind a child's inarticulate litany of desperation.

Light came on, created the world, froze my face. Instantly, I was safe.

Elfield took his hand from the light switch and caught me as I toppled, wrestled me back onto the couch.

Nauseated and weak, I was safe nonetheless from that terrible dread because I could confront the world on my own terms. The light, cool and brilliant from its concealed sources, put shadows in ordered perspective, gave them form and purpose, made of them benches and masks and couches and instruments and other human beings.

Exorcised by knowledge, the phantom voices were gone, leaving me the pounding of my heart. The curdled juices of my belly subsided into dying broken waves. The light had banished the horror of a universe without boundaries.

I stayed where Elfield had let me drop, arms by my sides, breathing a ragged snare staccato. And I saw the wicked elegance of what he and the woman had done to me. For what had occurred was not so extraordinary. It was as commonplace as fever, as true nightmare. Ah, Rimbaud. Only its shocking suddenness was novel. And that difference was the difference necessary to focus attention on a condition which all the artifices of humankind had contrived to deny and disguise and revile.

"You see, don't you?" Sriyanie was near me, warm, human, and caring, touching my hand with compassion. "That was what we wanted you to remember."

Footsteps came with incisive clarity across the laboratory. Elfield held out to me a gnarled dark shape. The strength of flint-worked timber tremored in my hands as he pressed the mask into my grasp. I gazed wonderingly at it, understanding.

"Our ancestors were there," he said, "for perhaps three million years. And we're still there, for all our cerebral abstraction. I hope it's quite clear: men and women did not invent gods and fall in sudden awe before them. They were crushed by dread and splintered that insupportable terror into fragments less likely to overwhelm them. They restrained the gods when they fashioned them."

I turned the demon's face in my hands, and the ambivalent victory of those ancient shamans piped all around me a melancholy fugue.

I closed my eyes. Fatigue drained the resources that light had lent me to dispute the dark torrent.

Elfield's words sifted through the crevices of my drugged exhaustion like crystals of ice.

"This culture has been betrayed by its own energy," he said. "There is a flaw in our time so grotesque that we leave its reckoning to charlatans and prophets. Marguerite, that malaise underlies sexism, racism, and exploitation of every kind."

Elfield's syntax fled past my weary mind, all but eluded me. Urgency began to mount and demand the sense of his statement. Sriyanie was a flare burning near me. I reached for her hand, gripped it against me.

"In large degree," the voice was saying, "the central wound of our time is singular and peculiar to this century. It is a crisis of consciousness. Peoples have known it before, yes, but never so widely nor so intensely. Marguerite, humanity is failing because we have failed to take the future into our hands."

And our future is our past. The hard edges of the demon mask, still clutched by one hand against my side, scored my flesh through my dripping blouse. The flux which bound me to the others demanded recognition. I was turning inside out, lungs and womb and bladder functioning beyond the membrane of skin which marked off my body from the universe. We three human beings were the echo of some archetypal triptych which advanced out of the grid of eternity into the cycle of Elfield's statement and the damp contact of Sriyanie's hand in mine.

I knew change, and put it in order, and fell in that moment in anguish and supplication before what it signified, and the burning mesh of meaning and power tightened about us.

Elfield's voice was chill, didactic.

"The practice of science calls out our best qualities, but finally its products crucify imagination in the name of immediate utility. We are caught in the moment when the noosphere, the human realm of mind, has turned back in incest on itself. We've burnt out the resources of myth which might have given us metaphysical direction."

Yes.

"We work efficiently, so that we might consume in comfort, and the spirit of our work is poisoned. There is no satisfying achievement in it.

"Our repositories of human encounter with fear and hope are drained of meaning. We have yielded ourselves to the machine. Certainly religion has failed us. It is alien to the possibilities of our age. It is too firmly entrenched in regimes of idea and emotion long voided—castes of privilege, gender, imagination."

The humming pulse came up out of my heartbeat, stretched and stretched, and its tension would not break or falter. I might have been upon a rack.

"Still, there is dread and exultation locked in our culture's belly. It is not supernatural, as the old mythmakers pretended, but *transnatural*. We are pitiful in the face of the immensity of the universe. Yet our possibilities are truly limitless."

He fell silent. I could hear my blood laboring. I opened my wet eyes to the bright light and saw only swirling forms without meaning. "Marguerite," the dark man said, standing now behind the white-haired woman, his hands lightly on her shoulders, "the bond of time can neither be propitiated nor ignored. Only embraced."

They helped me to my feet, and we went out to the quiet coolness of the rock garden. The sun cast fantasy about the western sky and a soft breeze made the gray pebbles fresh and timeless. The four blooms were cupping their fire in upon itself. I stood in the breeze until the sun was gone.

* * *

THE JUDAS MANDALA

We dined in a small, high-ceilinged room hung with faded cloths of Arabic ancestry, suffused in golden light from a pierced-metal pendent lamp. In the middle of the carpet a beautiful beaten brass tray stood on low cypress legs inlaid delicately with tortoiseshell. A copper bowl rested in its center, and a flask of rosewater. We sat on cushions, and I glanced with faint unease at a manila-bound manuscript lying near the edge of the table. Elfield brought a tanaka of steaming, aromatic coffee from a small brazier in a corner of the room and filled our tiny china cups. I felt a momentary regret at refusing Sriyanie's offer of a batik robe; my tattered jeans were an unnecessary discord. I picked up the folder and saw that it was my M.A. thesis.

"Jesus," I said, flipping it open. "You're really raking up the dirt. How the hell did you get this?"

"*The Anti-Bodhisattva*," Elfield mused, sipping the froth from his cup. "Ingenious, Marguerite. A trifle arbitrary, though, for a poet?"

"They were specializing in critical ingenuity that year," I said. "I play by the rules in examinations, doctor. Otherwise, why bother? You got it from the English Department archives?"

"You undervalue your insight. Thank you, Teddy." The bruises were fairly repulsive, and the man looked sourly at me as he put down bowls of falafel, baba ghanoush, cold stuffed vine leaves, and small cubes of white cheese. I tensed, but it seemed that preprandial gymnastics were not on the agenda. I winked at him as he limped out, and his lips twitched. "I obtained it from Professor Fletcher," Elfield said. "His memories of you are ambivalent."

"No doubt," I said. "The old pig tried to get into my panties the first day I turned up at his course. He doesn't like women who answer back." Lemon and garlic cut the smoky flavor of aubergines; I ripped the ta'amia and dug in for more. Sriyanie smiled at my hunger and offered a bite of vine leaf; I licked her finger as I took it.

"Fletcher and I were students together," Elfield said. "It's not an association I relish, but it has its uses. He has vivid recollections of your mother. He's been trying to locate some of her poetry for years."

I laughed coarsely. "My mother? He *must* be senile. I'm the black sheep, David. My family are stunningly illiterate, even by the standards of the most fervent holovision executive."

The psychologist poured water over his fingers and took up the folder. "I fear I've had time for only a cursory glance. Do you think Vonnegut will get his Nobel this year? He's on the short list again, you know."

"If he does, it'll be for his second period," I said. "This only deals with his early work, up to the time he almost abandoned *Breakfast of Champions*."

"He's become too much the bodhisattva himself," Sriyanie said. "One expects to see white light shining from his face. It's a risk you may run yourself one day, Maggie."

My mouth was full of tahini and bread; I raised my eyebrows. "Nobody reads poetry, Sriyanie. I don't think I'll hold my breath." Elfield passed the folder back to me, open at the epigraph. Alan Watts. My eye flickered down the page:

> The adult or mature version of primal narcissism is, of course, "cosmic consciousness," or the shift from egocentric awareness to the feeling that one's identity is the whole field of the organism in its environment. But if this is not to remain a purely contemplative state, if, in other words, the liberated man is to return to the world like the bodhisattva, he will seek the means of expressing his sense of being "at one with the whole world in pleasure and love." Because the means are aesthetic, his approach to the world is, as Marcuse suggests, that of Orpheus, "the priest, the mouthpiece of the gods," who tames both men and beasts by the allure and magic of his harp. . . . For in the value system of civilization the artist is irrelevant. He is seen as a mere decorator who entertains us as we labor. . . .
>
> The liberative artist plays the part of Orpheus by living in the mode of music instead of the mode of language. His entire activity is dancing, rhythm for its own sake, and in this way he becomes a vortex that draws others into its pattern. . . . The high art, the *upaya*, of the true bodhisattva is possible only for him who has gone beyond all need for self-justification; for so long as there is something to prove, some ax to grind, there is no dance.

THE JUDAS MANDALA

I glanced up as Teddy leaned past me to retrieve the empty bowls. He replaced them with lamb brochettes and more tahini, the glistening olive oil brown and red with cumin and cayenne pepper. Elfield poured more coffee, thick and very sweet. The liberative artist, I thought, plays the part of Lévi-Strauss by living in the vocabulary of eating. . . .

"I'm impressed by the deft way your interpretation inverts the notion of genuine sanctity," Elfield said. "If the most intransigent characteristic of human existence is the search for purpose and significance, the limit cases are the numinous and the nihilist—"

Nihilistically, I gibed, "Apocalypse and *absurdité*."

"Indeed. But don't you have a mandala there, the two faces in one surface of a Möbius strip? I've always been intrigued and appalled by Plato's proposal that society ought to contrive a magnificent binding myth that carries conviction for the whole community. That would certainly seem the burden of *Cat's Cradle*."

"Well, consider it in tandem with *Sirens of Titan*. There's a mandala for you. Have you ever noticed their frontispiece disclaimers?" I searched quickly through the notes at the back. "Yes. 'All persons, places, and events in this book are real.' Very droll. Then: 'Nothing in this book is true.' It's quite flagrant. Vonnegut has us by the throat, so we choke while we laugh."

"Intellectual jokes," Sriyanie said, nodding, "and in bad taste at that. The bitterness is so gentle it almost makes you cry."

"Yes," I said. "Like Heller. The watershed between pain and laughter. Well, I tried to locate the general structure of his intention. In one of those two books he offered a putatively liberated man in a world that's vastly and cruelly ordered. In the other order is a facile myth in the midst of rampant anomie. That's why I employed the idea of Taoism. Spontaneity can't be forced or it becomes deliberation. Yet out of spontaneous lawlessness comes the ineluctable Tao, serenity in absurdity, transcending itself into an integrated unfolding."

The brochettes were cooling; I shut up and ate. The psychedelic horror of the afternoon returned to haunt the room. There, indeed, I had touched some flawed Tao. What was I doing here? The situation was insane. These people had instructed their retainer to assault me; now they presented me with food and drink and solicited my literary opinions. And Elfield had placed a large, unearned amount of money in my bank account. I looked at Sriyanie; she was regarding me with an emotion so apparent I could hardly give it credit. Teddy returned, placed before us a huge silver bowl of rice and chicken, prunes and apricots and raisins. A tang of ginger and spices rose from the stew.

"My own recipe," Elfield said, smiling, "though it's based on a tagine recorded in the *Kitab al Wusla il al Habib*." I raised my eyebrows. "A manuscript dating back to the Middle Ages."

"You eat well, doctor."

"Of late," he admitted. "When my wife was alive, she insisted on preparing most of the food herself. It was a reaction, I suppose, against the gibes of the antifeminists. Her cooking was abominable, I fear. Since Jean's death I have given over the care of my belly to Teddy and discovered a belated interest in cuisine. My involvement in the preparation remains, I confess, a rather scholarly one. Tell us more about Vonnegut."

"Well, I don't know if Vonnegut had any of this in mind when he wrote, but Rumfoord is clearly the very mirror of the bodhisattva-artist, skewed and reversed. He's certainly the mouthpiece of the gods: he predicts the future with absolute accuracy. The chronosynclastic infundibulum has placed him beyond all need for self-justification, and indeed his entire activity is dancing. He dances a spiral from the Sun to Betelgeuse, he dances over his golden jungle gym in Newport, he danced to the leitmotif piped across the light-years by the Tralfamadorians."

"Cosmic consciousness!" Sriyanie said in delight. "He's been liberated into ubiquity by the infundibulum."

"Yet his characteristic adjective," I pointed out, "is 'punctual.' In his 'enlightenment,' he instigates deceit, death, and destruction—and as a final irony, he never learns how paltry the ends of the robot messenger are."

I fell to eating, and my mind winged away into the cruel artifice of *Sirens*. Vonnegut shimmers with doppelgängers. I thought of Malachi Constant, the man who yearned to carry a "first-class message from God to someone equally distinguished": a tiny analog of the whole human race, which had labored for its history to carry a spare part for Salo's damaged spacecraft. And humanity itself is merely an analog of the robot, the messenger designed for absolute efficiency, durability, and reliability, still on the job after eighteen and a half million years.

The book aches with lies and deceptions. With Salo's assistance, Rumfoord designs The Church of God the Utterly Indifferent. Its motto, "I was a victim of a series of accidents, as are we all," is precisely, and on an unimaginable scale, what we are not. Its practice is the essence of fraud.

When happiness ensues, it has equivocal roots. The woman Bea, when at last she transcends her spurious dignity, retains no linear identity through which to rejoice in the fact. And the final, touching scene is illusion. Unk is not what Malachi Constant was—aggressive, loud, childish, wasteful—but neither is he a man. He dies in illusion, as programmed by hypnosis as any computer.

The book, I brooded, folds back into itself like a box of mirrors. I found the quotation from the very beginning: "Everyone now knows how to find the meaning of life within himself. But mankind wasn't always so lucky.... Only inwardness remained to be explored."

"Inwardness . . ." I muttered. "Is that what you're intent on exploring, doctor? Are you seeking the fifty-three portals of the soul?"

Elfield picked at a chicken bone. "There is no great distinction," he said, "between the inner and the outer. We are a field. Empathy is all. Are you thinking of Salo's message?"

" 'Greetings,' " I quoted.

"It could have been: 'War!' "

"In America," I said, "it is."

"And what of *Cat's Cradle?*" he pressed. "As I understand you, you're arguing that nobody's as malleable as the man who's persuaded that his life is undetermined. Yet Bokonon preaches the reverse—that we are all constituted into teams, doing God's bidding unaware."

"Precisely. And that myth permits the destruction of the world through sheer irresponsibility. Dr. Hoenikker, the man who invents ice-nine, is a monstrous image of the bodhisattva. He's the very spirit of spontaneity, Tao in flawed action, the unconscious without an ego to direct it. Life is *Maya,* the Great Game. Unfortunately, Hoenikker's games include inventing the atomic bomb and ice-nine."

"So nobody is as negligent," Sriyanie said, "as the man who believes his actions to be totally ordained."

"But isn't this the paradox of the *true* bodhisattva?" Elfield said teasingly.

"I don't know," I told him. "Watts says, 'Not caring is the parody of serenity.' "

Just as I had convinced myself that I could eat no more, Teddy brought us crystal bowls of muhallabia. The pudding was smooth and cool on my tongue, tasting faintly of orange blossom. I pressed fragments of almond and pistachio between my teeth, releasing their stronger flavor into the sweet milky rice. My hand touched Sriyanie's; she clasped my fingers. I felt exhausted. What were they trying to tell me? This was, in some way, a ritual of preparation. It seemed unlikely that our discussion of mid-century classics was an accident. Yet my interest in Vonnegut's work was itself quite fortuitous. Were we a karass or a granfalloon? That question, of course, possessed a circular invalidity. I snorted in self-derision and dropped my spoon into the empty bowl.

"Here's your mandala, doctor," I said. "The inevitability of illusion, and the illusion of inevitability."

He smiled, and poured us each a final cup of coffee. Sriyanie leaned across and put her head against my arm. She turned her face to me. She whispered, *"Ami du criminel."*

FIVE

I opened the bedroom door, wanting her, my left hand on her hip, and she turned like a soft leaf bending to inexorable gravity, away from me, and her mouth said, "Good night, Maggie."

I would not believe it.

Let your feet fall as they will and they serve you well enough. Walk on gravel, pavement, broken soil: the gears change, your balance shifts and knows its own decent habits. A stairway? Limbs rise and fall a little differently, the juices are called a trace more quickly. A pothole? Avoiding it takes some attention, but you do not question the fidelity with which thought becomes action. Doubt that intuition and you are becalmed. It's the same further up the scale.

My hand clamped on her flesh in painful outrage.

"Sriyanie, stay with me," I said, and found I was scarcely breathing.

Her face was pale in the albinism of shock. I could not then gauge how curious that was, for she had lost none of her composure. The dazed, excited touch of pseudo-fever had not quite left me.

"No." Her hand stroked my clenched fist cunningly, and a white-hot nerve jerked my fingers from her thigh.

THE JUDAS MANDALA

I went back through the half-opened door, into the matte black room, and wondered why she stood gazing in pain, the white welt on her leg flushing with blood. Her pain was not from my hand.

Eventually she said, "Something has started, Maggie." I waited, leaning in the half dark against the door. "I can't tell you what it is. Try to come to terms with it. We'll talk in the morning."

She took one step, pressed my limp hand against her warmth, and went away.

I kicked off my clogs and stabbed switches at the side of the low bed until a faint white illumination came up to etch the room. Dropping clothes as I moved, I lit a cigarette and climbed between the silky sheets.

A hot conviction of change ambled along my nerves, lolling its tongue. I crushed out the cigarette, astonished, and hugged head against knees.

The thought lashed, caught me between nape and midspine, stretched my mouth wide in a shout of anger and fear.

She is protecting—

And then there was then no break then in the thought then that then and then and then looped out and grasped its own tail then and ran its course neither faster nor more slowly than any other outraged thought, yet sinewy in its midst was the unmemory that

—SPLICE—

(Hunched naked in the sheets I felt a breach, a fissioning that started behind my eyes and in my lungs. A vast deep gonging splintered streaming light, pure tones and radiance at the polyhedral faces of the splitting room. Bones cracking. Teeth drilled to the nerve. The infinite curvet down a spiral of Lobachevski diminishment, Zeno's endless race.

And Time stopped utterly.

Blackness was all, anesthesia; the universe itself had gone.

A Presence cupped me in my nothingness and made utterance. I knew It as It spoke. I paid heed, I took action as It directed. And then I expunged my memory of It.

Is it possible to recount what occurred? Even now, when what then was blotted from memory has been recovered to me, is it possible to render it in words? No. Can a mystic tell of that secret vouchsafing which is torn from her in its every essential when she takes on once more the flesh and its limitations?

In that timeless void, prepared only by Sriyanie's ambivalent cruelty, I confronted a fact so large that I heeded and rejected it in the instant of its disclosure. The Presence burned like plasma into my soul. In that protected place It wounded me with Its joy so dreadfully that my shrieking mind sought to smother its sweet pain, as one might crush a flame or a rose burst forth from one's own breast.

In the void, the Presence spoke in the voice of a thousand pealing bells:

—Marguerite, my child, my ancestor.

"Yes . . . Mother?" Can God be one's mother?

—You suffer.

"Yes."

—I regret the need for your pain, but your destiny is to suffer still further.

"Must I?"

—I shall not impose this suffering on you, Marguerite. It must be your choice. You must accept it.

"Yet you say it is my destiny."

—There is no predetermination of fate. Destiny is choice.

"Some choices are better than others."

—Yes.

"Tell me what to do, Mother. Daughter."

—Sriyanie needs you. Go to her.

"I don't understand. She's here, in the house."

—True. She is also in another place, another time, and in danger. Go there. Lend her your aid.

"Go to . . . another *time?*"

—You know how. Search within yourself.

"Mother, I shall do so. Tell me, is David Elfield part of this . . . destiny?"

—A crucial part, no less important than you, than Sriyanie.

"More important?"

—No. You are linked, you three.

"What must I do to aid them?"

—You will know, when the time comes.

I bowed my head in submission.

THE JUDAS MANDALA

—Go, then. I love you, child.
"And I you, Daughter. Mother. I love you, love you."

The void closed about me and was Nothingness. The flame was locked within me and forgotten.

Time began. I did not know that it had stopped.

Two dark-clad men stood brooding in the frames of Kirlian blue, searing violet.

I stared into the ruptured net of spacetime, stared without belief. They were there. They were real. I sat there on Sriyanie's silky sheets and sweat burst out on my naked body.

In their grasp between them bulked a thick gray metal ovoid so weighty their shoulders bunched and bent toward it. They studied me amid the fractioning sections of my overloaded senses. Their pale wide features were frozen into masks of pity and trepidation. The taller man took the mass of the thing more firmly against his thigh, freed one hand. He touched a contact on the curdled metal.

I was entirely vulnerable, bare flesh hue-splashed in the demolished spectrum.

Something deep within me thrust up shield and sword.

Cylinders of energy so bright they were blindness blinked. . . .

Bent back in the curve of time reversed, blazing in an instantaneous self-consumed inferno.

And like a tight-bound spring explosively released, I was slammed back to that first nanosecond of interrupted perception—

—SPLICE—

My eyes burned, not in the terror of the peeling spiral of anachronism but with the shocked afterimage of intolerable brightness. I had turned it back (*would* turn it?) against the intruders, had seen them blacken through that other blackness of sun glare.

Muscles tensed; I knew horror and confusion and the scent of hot copper in my sinuses. There came, as I hunched in the sheets of the bed in Elfield's mansion, a breach, a fissioning—

—SPLICE—

I fell into time broken, space splintered.

The surfaces of light collapsed about me. A chill breeze

THE JUDAS MANDALA

goose-bumped my skin. Still naked, I was standing in a grimy open square, gasping and gagging at the foul air, legs bent, facing five men in dark identical garb. Weapons came up in their hands. Their eyes were intent. There was an alley straight ahead of me in the moonless, lunatic night.

I hit the alley at a dead run.

The putrid stench caught at the back of my throat and mixed with the stink of my own sweat. It hung swirling on the air in an almost visible miasma from the back of an ancient market, ruined and abandoned, from crumbling tenements eroded by the airborne acids which stung my eyes, from some sluggish oil-ripe waterfront. I ran, almost blind in the gloom, feet thudding on the broken asphalt of the paving.

The air crackled, and an explosion of white-hot brick and stone sprayed out of the dark wall at my left. Blood welled from my grazed face and stung my left eye. I leapt and feinted, programmed by my Attack instructor's lessons, stones cutting my feet, and snatched a quick glance over my shoulder. A flare of light hissed past my head.

Abruptly there was a lesser darkness at my right hand. I seemed to scent rather than see it. I hurled myself forward, right hand thrusting, grasping, pivoting on the crumbled wall. For a timeless instant my body hung unsupported, left hand outstretched before me. Then I hit the moldering rubbish piled against the far side of the wall, slipped, slammed sideways to the ground. I got up again, teeth clenched against the desire to scream, and limped into the blackness of the market.

It's the drug, I assured myself. *I'm still lying on his couch. Jesus, I can see why they were banned.*

I also knew, absolutely, that it was real. Still, a part of me wanted just to stop, to close its eyes and wait for all this to go away. I pushed between plastic boxes and damp sagging plywood. My skin crawled with filth and the cold, and tiny hairs stood on end. I stopped, breathing with immense difficulty, and let my muscles slacken for a moment.

Real or imaginary, why *shouldn't* I close my eyes and make it all go away? That was how I had got here.

I forged images of geometric dislocation and tried to suck the singing forms of smashed color out of myself.

THE JUDAS MANDALA

Nothing happened.

I started to shiver, to shake convulsively. Tremors chattered my teeth together.

Feet slammed in the alley. Hoarse cries in some foreign tongue broke rudely into my spiritual disintegration. Above me, through the lattice of rotting plastic and rusted metal struts, a white explosion of flare light hung, slowly fading to blue. Twisted roof metal, punctured with nail or staple holes, splattered light in momentary molten gobs all about my feet. Close behind me someone shouted, and a pale beam ripped a tremendous jagged welt along the wall near my head.

My mouth filled with a bitterness of indecipherable words. I spun, shot out my arm. Middle knuckle crushed throat. It's not Teddy, I thought foolishly. The weapon glinted out of his grip to crash amid rubbish. His face, when I rolled off his shoulders, recalled Sriyanie's: the same pale quasi-negroid features. He would no longer have a voice, if he woke up; blood ran from his slack mouth. Sickened, I jostled him around, searched his clothing for some clue to this madness.

There were no papers, no credit card, no coins, no keys. He was not even carrying a handkerchief.

Everything was very quiet. No lights at all remained. Only the stink of terminal pollution.

A deep, deep purple beam came into the sky, sweeping toward me, truncated in some impossible fashion halfway between me and its unseen source. I squinted in the freezing gloom and saw—something—hanging there at the end of the beam, wafting with controlled precision toward the market. I cowered, knowing threat and nothing of its nature, feeling my guts and bone and flesh shrinking from the thing as the beam carried it in an arc to hover a hundred meters from me. The fabric of my cells felt its pressure pushing from within at each conjoined membrane. Teeth ground tongue raw and my whole body crashed into cramp and

—SPLICE—

Hunched in the sheets in Elfield's house, muscles flawed metal, naked and spiritually battered, I felt a breach, a fissioning that started behind my eyes and in my lungs.

Spasmodic retreat carried me from untime to the source, finally, of that other wonder I had glimpsed under the drug: the shrill bright web which wound Elfield and Sriyanie and me in a swathe of eternity. The certitude of that potency, that absolute conviction, came up about me like a comforting mantle) and the thought fled out of its loop and ran its course—

protecting me. She is protecting me!

Anger jerked my head up, went through deltoids to clenched fists. She had refused to sleep with me because she did not believe that I could protect myself. Somewhere she was standing guard on my behalf. Against what? It didn't matter. The point was that she had not trusted me sufficiently to tell me. I kicked the sheet aside.

And unmemory cascaded into consciousness, scattered the tinder of my brittle dignity.

I stumbled against the bed. I touched my cold, dry face. There was a place of wetness and the smarting of grazed skin. Liver blackness shone on my fingers in the gloom, clotting fluid, and the flushing itch of flash-radiation sunburn scratched across my flesh. I could not breathe. I went down across the bed into an emptiness beyond any awareness of my profane stigmata.

The hall was silent and empty. "Sriyanie!" I stood in my nudity and panic, yelling to no echo. "Elfield, you bastard!"

Jaw clenched behind upper teeth, I shook my noise-filled head like a wounded beast. Nothing moved below me. No flying footsteps to my need. Perhaps, I told myself, there is nothing they *can* do but wait.

I turned back into the room. I picked up my blouse and jeans, hand fairly steady, dressed, and took thought.

Item: the rules have been changed.

Or had they? I rubbed the abrasion on my cheek, checked the scratches and bruises on the soles of my feet. My thoughts kept creeping down the path of dank atavistic archetypes.

It was as though I'd slotted a key into some set of universal laws, forgotten, perhaps, or undiscovered, as real and bizarre as quantum logic. That was not a terribly novel notion; the psi freaks and mystics, after their respective fashions, had been plugging it for long enough to take the edge of hubris off the concept. On the other hand, it was a favorite fancy of paranoid schizophrenics when they forgot to take their pills.

The sticky blood on my fingers brought a cough of laughter at that thought.

All right. The notion was blurry, but it had the virtue of eschewing ghosties and psychoses. Time broken, fractioning, looping, disgorging threat. The universe is a system, closed or open, describable without final consistency in *n* dimensions, with the capability of hurling hostile men in dark uniforms at a node we will call Maggie Roche.

No. The facts were there, but this way lay the never-never land of phlogiston and the luminiferous ether and "Benjamin Franklin Was A Rosicrucian."

So, item: Something is happening but you don't know what it is. . . .

The bitter refrain from Rabbi Zimmerman's classic song possessed a peculiar aptness. It also represented an abdication I couldn't afford. My philosophy prof had once said, "It is a trite conceit of the twentieth century that Gödel's theorem has confirmed us in our impotence. Nonsense. If any metaphysical corollary is to be derived from that feat of mathematical ingenuity, it is that we are heir to an unmanifest treasury." Curdled memories of time splintering and diminishing. A smile for null-E space. I shrink, therefore I am.

Item: David Elfield and the woman are in no position to help me.

Or, perhaps, they were already doing all they could to help me. Whichever was the case, they were keeping their distance and their own counsel.

Yet they had set me up for this chain of fantastic events. And their intervention was deliberate, not to say cold-blooded. Not (warm memories nuzzling) that it *was* necessarily cold-blooded. A rich harmony of passion and concern counterpointed the cool thoroughness with which they had precipitated me into this lonely crisis. Who are they? Who, for that matter, am I, now?

Item, appallingly:

Dear God, *what* am I?

And I knew what to do.

I stood, eyes closed, arms loose, and sought within myself. The regularity of breath. The deep cycle of pulse. The slight sway of muscle pitted against bone and viscera and muscle, against gravity, without vision. The faint susurration of fresh forced air through the room. The—

The new sense, barely recognized, pale and milky frail like wings of moth new-hatched in sun: the balance, the tough, delicate weighing of moment and minute, of Time through and beyond time.

Time opened to me like a sun-touched flower.

I gasped, face thrust up into the striae, a brief implosive exultation, a joyous fearful cry restrained to an awed breath straining. My hands reached out, imploring candescence shaped to the burnt taste of Time eternal howling in the yoke of each imperious instant. Here the vast tumescent torrent seethed, driving in the splayed dense yielding molten expansions and contractions of space eternal, matter generating time to spike the delirious geometries with flooding energy seeded flaring, birthing life, life catching up and weaving sweet chords and cords of space and time brought netted round a new echo of that mandala forged in the dreadful maieutic polarity, the Tree, the Yggdrasil.

And I was smiling, grinning, bathed in warmth and majesty, a child of time as well as space, my birthright power and dignity, the core of my every cell giving out its articulate message and mandate and instruction, the helix saga of two billion sun-circled striving: old mother-father, old artificer.

For a long moment I could not move in the face of that elemental clarity. And then, with a great bounding laugh, I ... reached out.

Time, energies burgeoning endless tension, bent at my touch. It folded, curved in before my pressure.

... Prometheus and the gods.

I was flung back, pain glaring blaring in me. The anomaly I'd wrought buckled, crashed over me, left me bruised and near to death.

The pain stopped, finally. In tentative near passivity I felt for the arching furrowed Timescape of the universe.

It was unchanged, lucent with glory. Its dynamics had rejected change, found again in one convulsive spasm its ineluctable shape.

"But that didn't happen before," I whimpered, like a child unjustly punished. Words came muffled, warm-wet-staggered against my mouth-crushing fists. Hard flooring hurt my left hip, even through the thick black carpet, and I realized that my face was thrust into the deep softness. The sense of time all girdling remained with me, its vast architectonics scored through my nervous system. I lifted myself to hands and knees, crawled to the bed, and let myself down on it gently.

Dull blue rings drummed wearily behind my eyes. My Attack instructor would not have been at all pleased. I rolled onto one elbow, wiped my streaming eyes, and blew my nose with resounding force.

I had ventured close to unwitting suicide. This Marienbad vortex would not be coerced without risk. I stopped thinking. The most primitive levels of defensive instinct had already learned some measure of control over this titanic torrent. And thinking paves the path to hell when your very reflexes are wiser than memory and analysis.

Although, the still small voice chided, there *are* concepts not unknown to science, Maggie, which relate action and reaction.

Okay. The blind man given sight must learn the laws of perspective before he takes up golf. Unsnarl a deaf man's cochleae and it takes a while for him to appreciate a nightingale, let alone orchestral Beethoven. I had floundered in the lesser ripples of infinity and had not drowned. I'd been cast up upon eternity's shores and fantastically had thought to compel its torrent.

My knuckles cracked white in my gripped fists. The wonder of it was that I still lived.

With delicate, tremulous care, I allowed the fringes of my consciousness to seek the universe which had opened to the gauche contact of my new awareness.

An urgency beyond my reckoning, a fork stirring my entrails, gibbered at the slowness which prudence demanded.

I held the impulse to recklessness at bay, explored my way with infuriated caution into the crystal vault of my own enigmatic totality, climbed the looming helix staircase of space carved by time.

Abruptly, with one of those jolts which make field of figure and bring backdrop leaping into central focus, the numinous terror of those awesome strata departed, left Time merely monumental. And in the neural certainty and pleasure and excitement of that adjustment to a set of temporal dimensions I had never known existed I took ... an infant's first step.

The green numerals of the bed's built-in clock flickered. Three minutes had vanished from the display.

Something akin to Coriolis vertigo snatched at me and contracted my stomach in brief nausea. I'd intended to jump back a full hour, but the habit of caution was branded too newly livid in my soul. Sitting in that dim room, I grinned with wild idiotic joy and sent the display dancing in instantaneous bounds like a Disneyland screening of *Last Exit to Brooklyn*.

I hadn't felt such incredulous exhilaration since the midwife handed me Megan's tiny bawling form.

Exhaustion cracked along my bones. I smothered a yawn, opened the door, and padded in bare feet along halls austere and ornamented. Whatever David and Sriyanie were up to, I needed the dawn air.

I trotted down a sweeping black-broken staircase, the beautiful handworked translucence of its carved curve gleaming even in deep shadow. An entrance hall gave onto a restrained minor forest, a place of cool fresh breezes and a marvelous tang of arboreal growth and fine loam. I wondered how a man of Elfield's avowedly radical temper justified such lordly indulgence. It bespoke a single-mindedness, the Faustian quality I had noticed initially, close to megalomania, like the American William Randolph Hearst and his castle at San Simeon, La Casa Grande. The reflection frightened me anew, put me on guard.

I was astoundingly hungry. Time travel, I decided provisionally, was plainly a high-calorie activity. Hands in hip pockets, I craved a basket of cold cuts and a bottle of Moselle, a moment of tranquillity to digest the enormity of the changes which had veined the quartz of my being. I had never before considered how pedestrian the needs of a true witch might be.

And that stopped me: no finesse, just sheer brute impact.

The fantasts do not begin to comprehend how monumentally demoralizing it is, on a sweet summer dawn, to know beyond the resources of laughter or arrogance that only one banal word can capture the traumatic essence of what one has become: *witch*.

The moon, far off in the west, seemed a faded heel mark on the sky's face. Cool and gray, the first tongues of dawn lapped at the purple jowls of the sky, acid eating at a cadaver formalin preserved. Faint coral bled anemic across the black-green treetops, and beyond Elfield's estate the broken teeth of distant city office buildings leered on the horizon. Sick with an indefinite weary loathing, I saw the pink pallid sky flick back to gray.

I held myself very still, putting a count on my breathing, until the thudding of my heart was just a heavy pulse in my temples. Shit, I told myself, if I can't control this thing I'm dead.

The pink light snared miles away on walls of glass, fled back to me in softened outline. I experienced an age-old paradox, the dislocation of thought and emotion: as if I were at once some nervous quivering thoroughbred and his compact pragmatic jockey. That touch of moral empathy calmed me like a cool hand on my brow.

Deliberately, I thrust myself back fifteen minutes.

Fine odors of timber and exotic floral scents mingled in a perfumer's rapture. Above, as I went forward into the wooded grounds, an arch of stars flickered, kaleidoscope-occluded by leaf and bough. My feet crunched half-dry fallen leaves.

The ground sloped upward to the left into broken, grassy runnels. I climbed to the top of a small hillock, and the pain of fatigue was a warm fluid in my limbs. Brushing twigs and pebbles aside, I let myself down in the cleared space against a bole and watched the horizon for the morning's third sunrise.

My eyelids drooped, and I slid into a drowsy reverie. Images scattered across my mind, advertisements for dreamtime. David and Sriyanie / leather and pale beauty / abstraction and flesh-scent warmth / dark uniforms and blazing beams consuming their source / a mandala spinning into gray light and coral rimming the crusted edge of eyes and horizon. The few clouds brooding above the bowl of heaven glowed into a richer crimson than the blood which had trickled from his slack mouth. . . .

The sun exploded at the horizon. A wave of golden light poured across the trees, flooding over gullies and

THE JUDAS MANDALA

verdure. The very tussocks of thick twisted grass took on the bronze, in that instant when light stood athwart them, of archaic swords and knives.

And the web was taut and singing, sun-bright wire wound about me, the hinted touch of Sriyanie warm and intelligent and David complex and strong, and Time whirled into the maelstrom of necessity called back

—SPLICE—

I came erect with the chill breeze starting tears from my eyes, my feet against cold stone in the small square. A white naked woman was running, and the chiaroscuro of that held moment captured weapon flare and the five figures leaping in pursuit black uniformed, the reek of decay like a membrane of slime across everything, the web whining in my ears and my own body plummeting through space to strike one man to the stinging gravel, time slowly shedding its reluctance, and above all the dreadful fact that I had been here before—that the naked fleeing woman was me and that I had to prevent myself from getting killed if I died in the process.

I laughed like a maniac, blood welling from my hands where gravel had scraped skin. There was another hiss of weapon fire and an instant of shocking silence marred only by the faint slap of the fugitive's running.

I lifted myself from the ground, knowing an imperative beyond reason or restraint, saw an arm coming, caught the heavy fabric and the limb beneath it, pivoted, let the body parabola across me. The other three men hesitated, their features drained in the jolt of double recognition. In a spasm of reflex they fired into the impenetrable shadows of the alley, spun back, and closed in on me.

Ducking, I snatched up the felled man's weapon, fumbled without success for its trigger mechanism, hurled it with ferocious force at the nearest figure. He screamed, clutched at his chest, and stumbled. I leaped high, slammed my foot into a peering face, felt cartilage give. A furious blow took me in the back as I rebounded; I howled, fell, rolled, fled away in the opposite direction from the alley.

I told myself: At least I've made it possible for her to get away. I was incapable of actually grasping my identity with the other running woman.

Rough, angry shouts in a fluid tongue. Behind the clamor of pursuit and fury the profound whining cycle was thrumming a pulse that sang with the pulse of my blood, gonging with two other cycles of calmer frequency. I smashed into a low marble column, the detritus of some nobler memory than this filthy quarter had known for decades. I tried to save myself but my wracked body could take no more. My outflung arms buckled and I collided with stunning force against a time-ravaged balustrade which collapsed about me in a spray of hard-edged bricks and rotten mortar. I curved my head into my breast, masked face with arms, and went down amid filth and agony.

Pounding feet slowed. The remaining functional nasties picked their way cautiously through the rubble, looking for me. There was a faint shout from the market as a flare stung the sky and stone exploded with a distant muffled crunch.

There was no sound at all when my prior doppelgänger killed the man who had fired the beam.

Dust fouled my tongue; grit bloodied bare hands and feet. I was close to total collapse, my body's equilibrium shaken beyond quick recovery. Muttered voice turned for the moment away from me, faded. In the red theater of my flesh was staged an anatomical tableau of desperation in extremis.

A gentian beam sprang up to score the graphite sky in the instant when, lost and anguished, I seized the skeined matrix which trapped me. The gently whispering mechanism of already thwarted death fell in its curved trajectory toward my earlier self at the moment when, with my last strength, I ruptured Time's pattern and took myself into its blackness.

Some enormous force—cold and ancient and calculating—caught me, Its potency mocking my futile exhausted struggles. It intercepted my retreat into the past.

The cadence lurched, hesitated at the lip of jangling noise, fell across the caesura of my act and the act of the Other, shifted then to the pulsar metronome of Time altered yet inviolate.

I lay sprawled on a vasty majesty of shade-flickered, flame-rippled marble, a splendid terrifying immensity of stone in one dimension. Tessellated geometry danced with images, broken only by a starlit golden bough, its upthrust branches folding round the delicate artifice of a metal cockerel, moon-embittered.

The crumbled, filthy square was gone.

I had not returned to David's dawn-touched forest.

Instantly, my life...

...blipped.

I was read, filed, edited.

The speed with which my appearance was registered and action taken was staggering. No warning, no hesitation.

I slept.

SIX

I slept.

A gorgeous, stately waltz of cellular renewal did *not* spin in terrible complexity before my gaze. I slept, and the unconsciousness of shock, overload, shifted to the relaxed balance of soothing rest. The beautiful precision of enzymatic reconstruction did not present itself for aesthetic appreciation. I slept.

Above me, in a room of mechanisms, I did not see the clear and radiant sky, sun dazzle softened by the polarized polygons of a soaring geodesic dome. Cupped in impalpable buoyancy, rocking airborne above bright metal convexity, I knew nothing. My eyes were closed, lashes meshed in the dark embrace of sleep, eyes motionless beneath still lids, not darting in the cryptic phantasmal vision of dream. I did not know the cycle of my blood and lymph which bore through the nets of vein and tissue their sparkling burden of artificial proteins. My chest moved to the measured rhythm of unconsciousness.

Asleep, how could I know?

I did *not* know. I slept.

PRIMARY: DATA GRID / OPTIONS
CONTROL: STABILITY: ORDER

SYSTEMS: SUBSYSTEMS: SETS
STRUCTURE: *static deployment of system's elements at each specified null non-null-entropy point in five-dimensional space/time*
PROCESS: *dynamic change in mass-energy or information along system's entropy cycloid*
FUNCTION: *teleonomic process of system's structure/environment transactional field*

Slumbering, I did not dream. Notions, concepts, ideas lay dormant in the balm of cortical inactivity. Major electronucleic changes ceased; I was asleep. I did not know the flickering radio/maser/partonic messages of machines in their superb toil. In dreamless sleep, I could not be aware of micron-thin jets of pressured spray piercing my flesh. I could not recognize the humming rapid motion of machines or the faithful autonomic quantal changes at my trillion synapses. I could not see the sun-shot fleecy clouds adrift in spring-sweet blue beyond the room's huge arch.

Rocking in air-soft fields of nothingness, I slept.

SECONDARY: PSYCHOSOCIAL
LIFE: *dysentropic steady-state open system*
MIND: *critical emergent homeodynamic living system, self-structuring at hypercomplex levels*
PSYCHOSOCIAL GROUP: *goal-generating systems of noetic ego subsets*
OMEGA: *hypothetical set of all systemic subsets, constituting ultimate goal-generating-satisfying nexus of all non-null-entropy five-dimensional space/time*

I slept, and sleeping did not dream, and dreamless did not:
perceive
think
know.
And yet—
And yet, Something saw the great room of medical devices, heard-saw-smelt-tasted (mirrored in the smooth and awesome minds of the machines) the shape and pattern of my torpid body; Something traced and comprehended the axiomatic grids of thought roaring within the burnished room; Something knew, in a kind of terror and

THE JUDAS MANDALA

furious excitement, that all this was real, important, crucial in some fashion I must grasp ... or I would die.

(And Something Else would die, Something Whose existence was so profoundly important I could barely—)

I cringed, shrank to a vivid point of outward-directed attention.

Unwaking, I unslept ...

TERTIARY: IDENTIFICATION SEARCH
DOMAIN SCANS: *No living female filling these parameters exists on file*
THEORETIC: *Physical manifestation consistent with Transit discontinuity*
ANALYSIS: *Unacceptable*
No available locus
No evidence of Transit energy effects
CONJECTURE: *Female possesses device capable of disrupting cyborg surveillance systems*
EVALUATION: *Probability: vanishingly small*
No evidence that female harbors known or unknown mechanisms within her body space
FULL FILE SEARCH:
Total search without prejudice finds 0.99999 brain/body signature identification with female, Marguerite Roche, 1970-2048, born Australia continent, poet
CONJECTURE: *If this female is Roche, her presence here implies one of the following:*
a) Error in files
b) She is a cryogenic subject revived by unknown oppositional group
c) She has been preserved by relativistic time dilatation in transit on a starship concerning which all records have been falsified

	d) She is an unsuspected immortal sport
	e) She is a genuine time traveler
	f) Other
ANALYSIS:	All listed possibilities except (e) imply unacceptable cybernetic failure
	Despite implicit disruption of worldview paradigm, alternative (e) is assigned highest probability
ADVICE:	I. RECRUIT & ASSIMILATE / or
	II. IMMOBILIZE / or
	III. DESTROY
	(Minimax option: IMMOBILIZE)

The poisons of fatigue were leached from my exhausted tissues. A howl of latticed feedback sang a harmony of dread in metal tones my tympanum could not register. I was unconscious in my floating bed, anesthetized against pain, cognition, memory, awareness . . .

Blinded, writhing without movement before concussion, I slept.

CONTROL: STABILITY: ORDER
(FACT / GOAL / ACT / FACT)
PROBE INITIATION BEGINS

Smooth baffles rose and covered my sleeping face. Curving, invisible fields sprang into existence, sought the slow cycled pulses of my brain, fell into resonance. Silent energies flared at the molecular level, poured tight toroidal ion currents through the trillion circuits of my nerves. The muscles of my back twitched, itched. I knew nothing of this rape. I was asleep.

PROCESSING
PROCESSING
PRO

And I was dreaming.
Images flashed, loomed, retreated . . . melded. Under

closed lids, my eyes jerked and scurried, scanning visions of machine-directed memory.
I dreamed.

A dollar bag of mixed candy always lasted me from the milk bar opposite school all the way home to the back gate. Inky fingers found the rustling bag every forty-five seconds, drew out a sweet, went to my mouth, dropped back to hold open the book which bobbed before my enchanted gaze, snaked up every twenty seconds to flip over the page. Eyes leapt, sucked magic from . . . Barsoom, Krebb's cycle, Knossos inventory tablets, Geller effect, Augustine's platonism, compression ratios, studies in anomie, DNA, Comet Jo, Lichtheim's pragmatism, Durrell's Alexandria, Bedford's country girls again, Hoyle and Wickramasinghe's life clouds; eyes darting, blurring, to footpath, paint-cracked fence, pregnant woman and brats crowding me (I *won't* be like that; shift to pass them, candy to mouth, cold breeze riffling word-encrusted pages), finding the line again, the words, the worlds. . . . I usually crossed the street on the imaginary diagonal which is the shared hypotenuse in the two lo-o-o-ng triangles forming the street rectangle from this block to that, reading, devouring, tossing away the tattered white bag at the front gate, thrusting the book in between class texts, opening the back door to familiar odors of *home,* yelling hello to Mum sweating over clothes in the steam-filled laundry, grabbing biscuits and milk, reading hungrily on the bed until Mum's footsteps sounded in the hall, sliding the book between mattress and bed base, counterfeiting diligent study of text . . .

. . . nursing all the time the bruise, the impotent fury for the grins on the turning faces behind me as I'd walked engrossed, the ugly contempt: "Goddamn little weirdo, reading *books* all the time! She can't even walk somewhere without *reading,*" the outraged bloody smirks, as though I were eating shit at their Formica dinner tables. . . . The sick pain . . .

CESSING
TRAUMATIC BLOCK AT CENTRAL IDENTITY MEMORY STORE

THE JUDAS MANDALA
PROBE CONTINUES
PROCESSING

Dreaming; hearing the impossible without ears attuned; recalling the unbearable without screaming; dreaming . . .

We had run, as best we could. My adolescent legs, skinny as they were, could have carried me to safety, but Nigel's alcohol-ruined constitution had no reserves left to spend. Clutching the poet's frail arm, lungs crying in pain, I stumbled along the glistening path. Too far away burned the faint neon tracings of a late-night shop. Behind, rubber soles slapping on the wet road, the louts were running.

We had come further than seemed possible. My breath jabbed. Nigel's glasses, streaked with rain and sweat, slipped and went under his thudding feet. He cursed, half slid on the greasy footpath, bent shakily to retrieve them.

"No!" I cried, tugging at his arm. "Leave them!" I dragged him after me, and we ran toward the red glow.

They were playing with us, running Nigel to an exhaustion of agony. His hair—long, gray, matted stringy in the drizzling rain—flapped about his shoulders. The splash of light bobbed before us, closer, but still too far, too goddamn far.

I started to scream, partly on principle. My voice came back strangely from the deserted factory walls. Nigel glanced at me with pain-blurred eyes, looked past my shoulder, stopped running, turned, thrust me behind him. Breath caught in my throat, chokingly. A leering face spat, laughed a high hysterical peal of idiot excitement. A hand shot out, slashed brutally at Nigel's mouth. The poet went down in mud and gravel.

"You fucking ball-less wonders," I yelled in rage and sickness. Uselessly I hit out, struck the one who held me a weak blow on the side of the nose. My hand glanced off the grinning moronic mask of his face. He snarled, then, and drove a fist up under my small breasts. I vomited at his feet.

Nigel was trying to get up. A fist took me in the back, a hand grabbed fabric and skin and spun me around against the old poet. We both went down again, blindly striving to protect our heads.

"Get up, slut," one of them said. There was no affect in

his voice. His face loomed, skin drawn tight over the bones beneath cropped hair, eyes vacant. Mud squelched under my hands. A car approached, throwing its high beam along the wet road. I hurled myself toward the gutter. The car slowed, blasted its horn, and ... went past, accelerating.

"Cocksuckers won't stop," boasted one of the kids, strutting. "Let's smash this long-haired bastard," he said. "Then we'll show this slag who's got balls."

I heard, faintly, through the torture of my lungs, the furious snarl Nigel made. "Let him alone," I sobbed. "He's an old man." A chorus of jeers. Boots flailed about us. I screamed stupidly as they killed him. Then they grabbed me and began unzipping their flies.

ALL METABOLIC SUBSYSTEMS HOLDING AND
   STABLE
R.E.M. RECALL FLOW HOLDING
CRUCIAL TRAUMATIC BLOC CONTINUES
ADVICE:
(Minimax option holding at IMMOBILIZE)
PROCESSING

Shapes of hurt, too coherent for dream, too vivid for memory—

Teeth bared, gritted in darkness, I stared blindly at the bedroom wall. Minute tremors at my back told me James was teetering between physical violence and self-pitying tears. (Self-pity? An emotion not quite remorse moved in my belly. Jesus the guy *loves* you!) He drew in air, harshly, as if to speak, then said nothing. I wanted to want to turn to him, turn without being forced to turn, hold him as once we had held each other: in wonder, joy, honest lust, compassion. I strained (the tensions in my body making their own equivocal statement) to find some fragment of empathy, and all I could discover was the thwarted, James-thwarting torrent of my own trapped freedom.

He turned over, and I knew he was staring incoherently at the dark ceiling. I could not move, could not, either, lie as I lay without displaying the most stupid, useless kind of boorishness. Grudgingly I faced him, aching with anger.

"Bitch," he said tensely, his voice demanding some impossible miracle.

THE JUDAS MANDALA

"Oh, Jesus, James." The words no longer exploded. "Don't start on that masochism bullshit again. You thought it was terrific when it was all theory. Do you really believe I'm just trying to castrate you? I can't be free if you put shackles on me and you can't be free if I allow you to. Sweetheart, let's try to—"

"Shut up."

I said nothing, trying to breathe as my Attack instructor had taught me. James turned some more, tentatively, and stopped; I knew tears were leaking down his face.

"Maggie," he said, "oh, God, Maggie."

In the little nursery, in the desolating night, Megan woke and began to howl....

BLOCK ON TRANSTEMPORAL ABILITY CONTINUES TO RESIST
PERIPHERAL TRAUMATIC OUTPUT HOLDING
TERMINATE PROCESSING

Clouds massed beyond the geodesic dome. The dreams were gone. Patterns of autonomic regulation made pretty ripples in brain, spine, tissues. Bright machines, surfaces glossy in infrared and ultraviolet, arose from their coven over my sleeping body and withdrew to service niches in the vast room. Their movement was noiseless: calculated, efficient. I lay in dreamless slumber. If Something other than my central nervous system observed carefully and with astounding prowess all that occurred, it was not the sort of Something which the mechanisms could detect. They settled into their places and took communal thought, brooding over my unconscious body. They did not know that they had been watched.

How could they know? I slept, senses locked in on themselves.

I slept.

CONTROL: STABILITY: ORDER
TERMINAL DATA:
I. *Subject may not be directly vulnerable*
II. *Significance of transtemporal block indeterminate*
III. *Minimax: Central Dissociation*
ENDS
PROCESSING

THE JUDAS MANDALA

PROGRAM FOR ACTION: RECRUIT & ASSIMILATE

Blip.

I awoke. I lay sprawled on a vasty majesty of marble, under stars, under the moon's bitter light.

From its spray of leaves, in plangent tones, the cockerel spoke to me. I was unaware that my life had been stopped, entered, rummaged through, restarted.

"Welcome, Marguerite Roche," cried the golden bird, and a bright chill sang in my exhausted nerves. "Welcome to Byzantium."

Terror drove me to my feet—

(Wraiths of light and shade trembled in the shifting air, shapes of men and beasts, flitting to a measured dance beyond my comprehension)

—but a fine incredulous intuition held me there, rocking on my toes and fighting laughter. Yeats, I thought, and if my thought had found voice it would have broken to a roar of mirth. William Butler Yeats, to the last grandiose archetype!

"Poet Roche," came from the gilded beak, cascades of jeweled sound, "welcome from death, from corruption, to the future."

My senses were lost in lunacy. I stood swaying in an immensity of hilarious madness. The gold sage in fire, holy fire; laughing master to my singing soul. Let's leave up the raveled knot of care. Sriyanie! David! Where is the meaning in this glut of words? Merely:

This is no country, I thought carefully, laughter bubbling, for young men, or edge-of-early-middle-aged women for that matter. Where are the young in one another's arms, birds in the trees at their song, flesh-and-blood birds for Christ's sake, the salmon falls, the mackerel-crowded seas?

Poet Roche? They know me? An eidetic flash of the torn-edged sheet: *JUVENILIA—The First Poems*. The slow sick empty whiteout of fear sucked away the laughter, and left me one moment of hallucinatory clarity.

"Hey, you," I yelled, my mind at some bitter, brittle extremity, "hey, thou golden cockerel!"

". . . honor, glory." The aural cascade ceased.

I honed a harsh whisper.

THE JUDAS MANDALA

"So *you're* the monuments of unaging intellect!"

Without shame, without anger, with no slightest awareness of my sarcasm, the thing gave a trill of pleasure.

"Yes, Marguerite," it cried, "yes, exactly. We are the immortal monuments of intellect. More than that: we are deathless intellect itself.

"And, poet from the dead past," it sang, while flames danced to the forms of living things, "we wish you to join us in eternal life."

"Well, then," I said, head nodding, "yes, that's very nice of you, extremely thoughtful." Little giggles spread like waves, like shock waves. "Neighborly."

"Poet Roche!" The tinkling voice rang resonant. "You are not well!"

"Huh?" My head jerked suddenly, up from the sucking gray whirlpool. "I'm— Sorry, what was that?" Through bleary eyes I saw the rigid metal face peering down at me. Does a nightmare know compassion and concern?

"The strain of transposition must have been very great," the cockerel said. Was it talking to me? The words blurred. I was lying on the tessellated stone. It was cool against my cheek. A flurry of metal wings clashed musically at the lip of oblivion. Wind fanned my brow, steel-hard talons stropped the marble floor. A pair of fiery eyes came close, gazing from a metal mask. My lips opened in a dry whisper.

"Nightmare! What are you?"

And the voice was hard, and sharp, and its music was the scything home of a guillotine blade. "Marguerite, you will know me as Daystar."

My lips twirked. I lifted one numb hand and waved it in a drunken gesture. "Daystar," I muttered, sliding into nothingness, "y've got a real nice little place here."

II
INTERFACE

Oh but he comes on tender
the fucker.
He's a lizard,
he's a lizard with a serrated tail
rasping his way
through a fancy dancing poetess.
Caring and love have
become blood and semen spattered
and coagulated all over
my abused body and my gothic imagination.

—Kate Jennings

SEVEN

A.D. 6036

Inevitably (and thus, the Lords being as they are, in its specifics diabolically casual) the summons comes for Sriyanie when she is most vulnerable, disarmed by a yielding passion. Drowsing, she's boneless and spent in the tangled tumble of her Five. Yuri turns slightly, nuzzles into the crook of Kolpias's heavy arm; his shin presses Sriyanie's gratingly, breaking her imaged reverie, and she too shifts a little, bringing her face around into the hairy curve of Guillaume's belly. The greater curve of the Blue Torus blurs in counterpoint. Guillaume's shrunken penis lolls in sticky fur; Sriyanie takes it in her hand and lifts her voice in a teasing, sweet soprano:

" 'Ah, sweet mystery of life—' " and holds the note until her voice shivers in tremolo.

Brolga prizes herself up from the knot, frowns, returns to meditation. Kolpias guffaws, his brutal chest shaking, and Yuri starts from sleep, snorts, sniggers as the note dies, grabs at Sriyanie's nose to blatt the rest. Guillaume gazes slyly down at them, retrieves his prick from Sriyanie's clasp and cups it piously, completes the line in creditable falsetto:

" '—At last I've found thee!' "

They all break up, even Brolga, and fall with one ac-

THE JUDAS MANDALA

cord on Guillaume, pummeling his naked flesh, grasping in threat and mock lust at the eponymous mystery. He wriggles free, springs to his feet, scampers with much display of terror to the sonic zone of the Torus and repels their attack with a lurid, deafening arpeggio. But Kolpias has him by the ankles and pulls him down; Sriyanie has found a kilo of fat crinkled peanuts and rains them on his hapless head; Brolga interposes herself in his defence, kneels, takes the mystery between her lips, reverently, and the mood is altered in a trice: Sriyanie is elevated in a daze of helpless love for these four. They cease their capers. Gently, they caress one another's flesh. The Torus is alert; its blue light softens and the tug of gravity fades: they float, enraptured and in love, and the Daystar enters their joy without warning, terrible and ineluctable, to bear Sriyanie away.

Here is the event's most dreadful aspect: she has known it will come, has expected it daily and hourly, and has denied it. Even in this moment of its actuality she backs off, trembling, bringing up her palms; some weak link of her will traduces her, saps courage from her perception of *what is;* the cyborg Lord comes to her from the Torus Transit locus and she shrinks away.

He pads forward proudly, imperious, claws glinting as they show and retract between white tufts of downy fur. He has the guise of a huge chinchilla cat, his eyes pale chrysoprase slit by vertical dark emptiness, stiff gray hair along the spine, tail thick and white, aloft, white as the dense, beautiful fur of his body. His voice wheezes and rasps: "Come, pretty one—come, child," and his tongue is rose pink and minutely scaled.

Sriyanie puts her hands by her sides and breathes. The Four of her Five are frozen in postures of hatred and resignation. She is the first of them to be called. Her waiting has not been extensive after all, yet she cannot believe it is at an end. Beth has prepared her; she finds herself unready. Her new love denies it, denies it.

The cat lifts on its back legs, half her height, and lays its paws against her. She does not recoil. "Sriyanie N'Zanvy, you are called. Are you ready for your season in heaven?"

Kolpias will hold back no longer. With an animal cry he lunges at the biofacted cat. The Lord whirls, rakes his cheek. The man staggers and falls, tiny globes of blood leaping in five lines on his pale flesh. The Daystar turns once more. "Woman, you will come. Let us leave this place with dignity."

She is not permitted to go to Kolpias. He sprawls unconscious in blue light, blood standing purple on his cheek. She would kiss them all, would weep; it is not allowed. She has been expecting this moment ever since the antiagathics technicians released her from the extended latency plateau. She is an adult; it is not forever after all. With their eyes the others make her promises she knows they cannot keep. *We shall wait for you; our hearts shall remember, and lay themselves open to your absence, and yearn for your return.* They believe what their eyes tell her, but she knows that it does not work that way. Her first love is lost, is stolen, is spoiled in an attrition not yet begun but inevitable. Her breast aches as she follows the cat to the locus; she chokes with grief. The shrilling of Transit makes her anew in another place, and the Four are gone; she is here and they are there, sobbing and raging, tending Kolpias's wound. Misery closes her throat and vision.

After a time she says, "You are inhuman. You are inhuman."

Four Nest adults stand at a respectful distance. In their faces is excitement and expectation. The cat lifts its great green-golden eyes to her and says, "We are transhuman, child. We are entelechies. Come, now, and greet your new companions. Your life has begun."

Already (to be blunt) I am straining empathy to the shearing point. Despite the prodigious informational access one has in holovision—the brisk, oblique summaries afforded you in vital color by macho, crop-haired pundits in their prime—it's hardly to be doubted that what one gains from the media is only marginally more than what one puts in. These observations and caveats, naturally, I write in the present, the final year of the twentieth century, *for* the present: the hazards of reportage in an open-ended context. If my words retain any currency beyond the present, matters presumably will be otherwise. The circuit is broken, for good or ill.

Nevertheless: the fact is, Sriyanie's *Dasein*, her being-in-the-world, is outrageous enough, but that of the Daystar's retinue is grotesque, unconscionable, even by her generous standards. In the full flood of Ontological Recap, it's true, I am Sri (and in echo am Beth, in attenuated echo am . . .) but shared memories meet their limits on that permeable interface where the *creatura* abstracts from the *pleroma*, essence in turn caving in from time to time **und**er the assault of radical existence, so that Will depasses Fact to retotalize Knowledge. Da-de-dum. Dear Jung, dear Schopenhauer, poor old Sartre. Let's leave it at this: *I'm* staring through a tiny crack in the wall, and *you're* straining to get some sense out of my muttered reports; we make use of what we can get, which is better than nothing.

So consider Sri in the Daystar's den, attended by the blithe sprites of the Lord's retinue, or six handfuls of them, at a time, in rotation. She's sullen and moody for a period, disdainful, uncooperative (and who can blame her?), but again we're in trouble. Neither Sriyanie nor the hivers count time as we do. We lack even a meaningful common chronology.

On the Outside, under the filtration fields, the Free people keep at least the rudiments of solar, lunar, sidereal cycles. But the world is long since razed to a monocrop of weeds amid filth, choked by millennia of high-energy waste, a catastrophic ecology of entropy. If their bodies still tick to the fluctuations and triggering jabs of that off-center precession, star and closest planets (an astrology long since assimilated in their biophysics), it is held of less account than the more intimate seasons of individual attainment: those quantal leaps of concept rehearsed by initiates in the fecund void of Timestop. Their yardstick is the Levels, a calendar relativistic as any starship's clock. In a sense they have returned to Sacred, as distinct from Profane, time; more accurately, it is Human rather than Industrial. It's a point we shall come back to in good time.

Bizarre? Unwieldy? Not by comparison. For the cyborgs' little doves and hinds time zings like an elastic band. Hook your head into teratotechnology, and the data bits fly with winged feet; galaxies zoom in your skull like randy bugs; or, if you prefer, primary partons grind to a halt, fuzzy in a dew of probability amplitudes, so that you may scale their crags and bounce in their pools. Time is, to all intents and purposes, obliterated. History is generating inside those awesome Central Processing Units so many googol times faster than fleshy cells can conceive that its human specification is without meaning.

Sriyanie's term as hostage/tourist/pupil in the cyborg domain comes (as for all Frees, borrowed briefly and replaced) at a critical period. On a rising curve into maturity, her trajectory has been interrupted. Everything shrieks at this violence, yet there is nothing palpable to repudiate. Anger fades; finally she is prepared to debate, at least, with her cloyingly sweet sentries.

"Your lives are a travesty," she tells Livani dully. He props his stained-glass chin on his knuckles and considers her tolerantly. "You are an abrogation of everything decent in myth and history."

"All life is a mockery," he says. Like her, he speaks chomsky; the internal dissonance of his statement squeals like a rusty nail. There are two opposed ways of reading this onomatopoeia. "Mind is the progressive escape from its substrate's deformations. Our logic nets are an attempt on the attainment of unshackled mind. The cyborg condition stands at the beginning of the route to freedom. Why do you let the laggard imperatives of your flesh blind you to reality?"

"But look at you!" she says crossly. "Intaglios on your flesh, like some goddamn ancient Maori, and you don't know what sensuousness *means!* You're riddled with contradictions, and you talk about logic. You've sold your Tao for a mess of frozen sophistries. I hate you—you are all disgusting."

Their teeth are white and perfect in the domain, but they do not eat. Her status being what it is, she is not permitted access to Transit, so cannot find escape even to the self-made menus of Timestop. What's more, it comes to her with horror that she sees no difference, in essence, between the consensus ontology of Timestop and the on-line fantasies of the Nest. If the cyborgs can fulfill your every need with pulsing fields juggling the fibers of your brain, a world of illusion tailored to your heart's desire, in what specific is this inferior to the synchronistic landscapes beyond the discontinuity door? Beneath her feet, in sturdy metal tanks, the bulk of humanity dreams: can her philosophy offer them more? She approaches a crisis of faith.

She seeks out Livani, homesick for her Four, and puts her arms about him. "Make love to me."

Near the first peak of her pleasure he enters her with wondrous skill, and they move in a delirium. When they lie exhausted—she tracing the tangled glowing flowers of his pale skin, he smiling gently at her astonishment—she says, "I don't understand. You're life haters. I don't understand."

"In communion orgasm is endless," he says.

Tranquillity is shattered; she pulls away from him, and numbness spreads in her body.

"You must stop running," he says in her ear without touching her. She refuses to look at him. "Very well," he tells her, "I shall try to explain. But this language is not well suited to it. The *only* way to know is to place yourself, in full trust, on line to the logics."

She wants to leave, but some terminal fatigue of the spirit drains her will. Eyes closed, unmoving, she waits passively.

"It is impossible to argue against the cyborg *Weltanschauung*. To do so would be absurd. The patterns they can manipulate so far surpass those we can command that we must take what they tell us on faith. And what they reveal is that life is a temporary, necessary aberration in the unfolding of a deterministic cosmos."

"Gigo," she says wearily. "The hoariest fallacy known to science: Garbage In, Garbage Out."

For a moment, the beautiful ageless man shows anger. Sriyanie has ventured close to blasphemy. He goes on, after a pause: "I've experienced its truth, Sriyanie. At the universal dawn, in the great White Hole, the metrodynamic was clear and linear and untarnished by Uncertainty. The cosmos told its time like a perfect clockwork, a sublime Newtonian machine. Cause and effect were simple and total. The intrusive blight of quantum probabilities had not yet arisen."

Dumbly, she shakes her head. His words are so close to the truth, as all effective deceit must be, but he has everything turned about.

"Inevitably, the planets coalesced about their suns, organic acids came together at their ice caps, amino acids formed as the enriched ice thawed, peptides, proteins, nucleotides—life. And the first disharmony intruded. Life multiplied, complexified, transformed the worlds where it was born, and introduced everywhere the randomizing horrors of its own holistic laws."

"No," Sriyanie says, aghast, "you're wrong."

"But mind came from life," Livani insists, more loudly. "The underlying order of the metric frame was discovered anew, and the possibility revived that it might regain its Laplacean grandeur. The cyborgs are that hope embodied: mind free of the organic pestilence which structured all five-space non-null-entropy systems into hideous irrationality."

Her lethargy is vanished. Deep within her some buried archetype lends her its comfort: Beth and her predecessors confronting this same vile caricature of truth. "It's insane," she cries.

How might she dispute with this emissary of omnipotent intelligence? The apodictic reality of Timestop is her bulwark. She *knows*, beyond authoritative denial or confusion, how the universe is hinged.

"Of *course* life structures the metric frame," she cries. "Of *course* it imposes constraints on the primordial condition. But that Ur-state is synchronistic. From the White Hole until the protozoa, the cosmic parameters interacted only by affinity! How else do you suppose that life arose? There simply wasn't *time* for the process to occur in your Laplacean fantasy."

"Child, child," Livani says softly, "do you dare to argue empirically with such mentalities? They transcend our boundaries so entirely that we cannot even keep abreast of the broadest generalizations from their real-time research."

"Endless elaboration of spurious, self-serving premises," Sriyanie gibes. "The constraints which thought impresses are syllogistic—exactly the paradigm your god machines function by. How can they escape the trap they've made for themselves? There's no niche in the Lords' mad world view for the basic data of human experience. You've been gulled, Livani. They've turned you into an adjunct of their circuits, and you can't allow yourself to recognize the obvious. If the Newtonian laws have some general validity, it's precisely because intention and value-ridden perception have *made* them work. It's only by profound inner silence, a stilling of the beta activity in your head, a retreat from will to wish, that the primal reality can reassert itself. You hivers stuff yourselves to overflowing with a clamor of contingent facts and relinquish magic."

"The goal of consciousness," Livani says stubbornly, "is the hypostasy of reason."

"The goal of consciousness," Sriyanie retorts, "is a harmonious equilibration of confluence and cause. Your culture strives to enforce predictability and you achieve nothing but a totalitarian extinction of all that's beautiful and loving in the universe. It is the cyborgs who are deforming reality, Livani. They have lust and no love."

"What do you know of beauty?" the man asks without sardonicism, radiant as a sun deity. "You play at patterns, while we soar on the Lords' wings into the cool tectonics of the All. I cannot tell you, little one—it is something you shall have to experience for yourself, when the Lord offers it."

She is sick at heart, corroded by his conviction. What is the foundation of her faith? A conventional wisdom obtained from eccentric puritans, an ineffable Mystery indistinguishable, if one is to be sufficiently ruthless, from the illusions she rails against. Sriyanie walks away from the hiver and crouches in her Black Place, desperate for Brolga's calmness and Kolpias's strength, hopelessly miserable without her Other and her Four. She shall be returned to them, eventually. She clings to this.

The cyborgs are not coercive, but there is an agenda, a curriculum of sorts. When she is not under her privacy field, deep in the meditation practices of Fourth Level, Sriyanie adopts some approximation of the Nest's observances.

Alien as they are, the hivers pursue their own perverse version of progress through the saccadic Levels. But they have for Other only the cyborg peripherals. So she meets no youths; all the members of her adoptive Nest are ageless adults. Among their delegated duties is custody of the region's Dreamtank humans. Nauseated, she attends their monitoring sessions. Another stint relates obscurely to the nurturing of those babies and children selected by the Daystar for full conscious existence. The hivers, of course, are functionally sterile; these infants begin their education in the womb of their dreaming mothers' Tanks.

THE JUDAS MANDALA

Shielded on an observation platform above the Nursery, Sriyanie stares in revulsion at a dozen neonates playing vivid Say-and-Fetch games with their simulation system. Almost immobile, their bald heads a third the length of their tiny bodies, they lie with one leg tucked up and the opposite arm thrown out, their field of optical vision constricted by the tonic neck reflex. Illumination in the Nursery is dim, as it has been since their birth; holographic helices coil and drift in the air. A robust, rollicking music fills the room, and voices speak to the babies in warm, uncomplicated chomsky. The pink creatures gurgle and cluck, their responses instantly shaped by the auditory feedbacks; but Sriyanie knows this is not the language they use to talk to one another. Machines of terrible subtlety are resonating to the patterns in their brains, mediating their dialogue, teasing and provoking and soothing them, a parallel system of limb and eye and larynx, conveying the building blocks of shape and texture and taste their own extremities are too feeble to obtain. The neonates are singing rhymes she cannot hear, with their electronic extensions; they are counting, adding and subtracting, as in the womb they once manipulated phantom rods and cubes and spheres drawn from their innate intuition codes by the probes of the machines. They will be weaned from this mediation, in time, as Free babies are weaned from milk; for hivers, Sriyanie reflects, that comparison is risible: their nourishment, with the exception of social potables, is rendered to them by means far more efficient than ingestion.

The case is similar, she realizes with distress, for all the other fathomless instinctual processes which link humanity to the beasts. For the beings of the Nest, it's true, breath and exhalation are governed by the ancient autonomic wisdom of the body; they enjoy the rictus of orgasm, its artful preliminaries and denouement; they are curious, creative, playful. But their instincts are given over to an egoic calculation so alienated from their juices that it is entirely reified in the vast coded energies of their cyborg masters.

Eating and drinking: gone, save as a ritual vestige.

Maintenance of body temperature and the comfort of the sensuous skin: abolished, shucked off to the care of a total environment.

Rest, sleep, dream: transcended, in the dazzle of endless day, all pity and terror purged at second hand by potent circuits.

Fear and aggression: forgotten in this garden of conciliation and unremitting generosity.

Excretion: unnecessary. . . .

She makes these lists and annotations constantly, holding herself to a stark detachment, itemizing clinically the lost dimensions of humanity. The Nest is patient with her, for their frustrations are obliterated in instant gratification. If they rebuke her in their inveterate pride, there is no hidden sting, no angry barb.

Sandstrom challenges her one day, with a serenity which denies any trace of belligerence.

"Sri, you can't claim you haven't learned a great deal while you have been with us." He speaks perfect Late English, and his accent makes her smile; she has been absorbing Mid-English from the teaching resonance.

"No," she agrees. "The pedagogy of the Nest is superlative. It is also addictive. I do not wish to be a programmed slave."

"You are inconsistent," he says. "Beneath your filtration fields Outside, do you hunt wild beasts with charred sticks and eat their flesh raw? Do you kill one another for a scrap of metal? Do you huddle in neurotic double binds of family and hierarchy?"

"That analogy's foolish," Sriyanie says. "One may learn and change. We have not abdicated from humanity."

"Are you sure? You are Fourth Level, Sriyanie. By the standards of those myths you love so dearly you're a middle-aged woman. Yet you are barely past puberty. Isn't this unnatural?"

"Even the australopithecines had a period of sexual latency in the growth curve, between the fifth and ninth years. How else could the learning brain retain its plasticity long enough—"

"Exactly! But your enzymologists have retarded that primitive latency plateau by twenty years. Neither of us is truly human any longer, child, if you insist on your mythic definitions."

"We have expanded our humanity, Sandstrom," she says heatedly. "You have discarded yours for a compulsive, voracious noetics."

THE JUDAS MANDALA

The dispute is trapped in its conflicting categories. Sandstrom leaves her at last, and she cleaves to her certitudes. By now, no doubt, the Four of her Five are dispersed across the world, separated, lonely, adrift in the appalling seductions of various Nests. Worse still (the thought pierces her), perhaps they remain together, loving and growing despite the suspended threat of severance; she is hardly ever in their thoughts; she is abandoned.

She will not seek out communion with the Daystar. She *will* not. She yearns for sleep, but it has been taken from her.

III

YANG

For science was founded originally on metaphor ... and the twentieth century has shipped metaphor to the ghetto of the poets. Consider: science began with the poetic impulse to treat metaphor as equal to equation; the search began at that point where a poet looked for a means (which only later became experiment) to measure the accuracy of his metaphor. The natural assumption was that his discovery had been contained in the metaphor, since good metaphor could only originate in the deepest experiences of a man ...

There is a danger in metaphor, however; the danger which is present in poetry: contradictory meanings connect themselves. So, science sought a methodology through experiment which would be severe, precise, and able to measure the verity of the insight in the metaphor. Experiment was conceived to protect the scientific artist from ambiguity.

—NORMAN MAILER

EIGHT
A.D. 6039

Jade in silver whorled the child's grinning face.

From sleep blank as death I woke into instant, startling clarity. Even so, as I lifted myself up from the floating crimson slab which was my bed, it took long moments to recognize that the chromatic swirls before me did indeed constitute a girl's face. Her giggles danced up and down a scale of tiny bells. Morning sun crossed my shoulder, splashed green and foil in her electrifying flesh, washed the white curve of wall behind her. Slivers of light caught at the lifted corners of her mouth, capered gaily with laughter. My lips parted.

"Hello," she cried, and darted forward. "I'm Trothy, and I'm so glad you're to stay with us." Her tiny excited hands flicked my sun-warmed shoulder, the hinge of my jaw, stroked my cheek like a butterfly's wing, flew down to grasp my hand as I lifted my right arm. "You're Maggie, yes, the Daystar told us all about you"—her eyes brighter than jade, with a silver filigree of lashes—"and we've read some of your poems"—mouth round and silver as she drew a quick gasp and shook her dazzling hair—"golly, it must have been scary in your time. Now jump up, lazybones, and I'll take you to meet the others."

"Whoa!" I laughed, the laughter surprised from me,

THE JUDAS MANDALA

dropping my bare feet onto the floor. "Slow down, Trothy. Let me catch my breath." I glanced about the unbelievable room, hand still tight in hers. Spirals of gentle sea-blue sparks wove a sculpture where the ivory wall, swooping around us in outrageous curves, bubbled. Solid chunks of stone jutted down toward our heads from the general region where wall became ceiling; a green-vined, hot-hued flower grew out of the ivory where ceiling became floor. Trothy gave my fingers an impatient tug.

"Um . . ." I swallowed, looking back at her. "Honey . . . where the hell *am* I?"

"You're in the *future*, of course," she said scornfully, and started to giggle again. "Not *our* future, that is—yours."

Yes. Yes.

My eyes closed convulsively and the world shuddered. That instant passed; the nausea was in my brain only, and I was sustained by that Something which was not wholly lost in this terrible absurdity.

"Hey, are you all right?" Trothy lifted herself on her toes, ruffled up the long hair on my nape. She looked concerned, then grinned her gamine grin again. "It *is* a bit unnerving, I guess. I admit *we* got a shock when the Daystar told us where you were from. But come out in the sun—the others'll be getting nervous."

She trotted gracefully toward the sun-filled, parabolic door. I stayed where I stood. Too many things were being thrown at my head too fast.

"Just a minute, Trothy."

I looked for a chair, failed to find one, sat on the floor and hugged my knees. The girl halted at the door, gave me a glance of quizzical, ostentatious forebearance, came back, dropped into lotus in front of me. Jade curlicues trembled, silver arabesques flexed with every movement.

"Maggie," she started, "all your questions—"

"In a minute," I said. Her quaint accent. She was evidently at ease with idiomatic English, which was startling enough in a child of so alien an era as this, yet the slight twang betrayed her. It echoed some tongue I could not place, and my poet's ear was troubled. Doubly troubled, since I *had* heard that accent somewhere before.

Sriyanie's cool, ironic voice.

I rubbed my jaw.

Confused, incomplete memories of what I had not seen as I slept, yet knew, trod forth. The machines had found me no less enigmatic, according to canons of their own which still half eluded me, than I found them, this world, the naked, beautifully adorned creature before me. There was comfort in that realization. I sought for the strands of the web which bound me to David, to Sriyanie, and they were there: a hum, a tactile sense subliminal as pulse. So I am not totally isolated, I told myself with a faint smile of reassurance.

The jagged fragments of pattern still hung unmatched in the void, but I could go no further alone. Questions and intimations nagged at the edge of my thoughts; I shunted them aside for the moment and got to my feet.

"Okay, Trothy," I told my small fantastic sprite. "Let's go meet the gang."

She giggled and jumped up with alacrity.

A broad grassy courtyard extended beyond the portal. Warm floral odors flushed the breeze; cumulus beasts pranced the sky. The wind's kiss reminded me of my own nakedness, and briefly I was reluctant to follow Trothy onto the grass. Don't be silly, I told myself. If a child hardly past puberty takes nudity for granted, it must be the fashion. Thick sensuous grass curled between my toes. A murmur of voices drew us around the curve of the ivory building, Trothy capering ahead.

Four superbly decorated youngsters, sprawled or squatting beside a purple-decked wisteria draping the ivory wall, turned their heads at our approach. They scrambled up, thronging around like puppies.

"Hi, Maggie, I'm Hibberd. We've been listening to your poems." Etched bronze, copper, highlights of gold. He touched my upper arm, bronze hair shaking light like molten droplets.

"Hello, dear." Koala soft, snuggling into me, her fur was blue as the sky. "I'm Itho."

"Hey, lady, that's a stark skin you've got!" At him Trothy scowled, and he blushed under the tawny gleaming scales that covered him like a suit of translucent coins. "No, really"—laughing and scuffing his toes in the grass—"I don't mean to be impolite, but we'll have to get you to a skinner."

"You've got a big mouth, Lior," Trothy said, grinning,

and hugged my spare arm. She caught the third girl by the hand and drew her in. Indigo ran waves of oil in the lava of her smooth skin. "Ziruthine," Trothy introduced. "She's sort of a poet too, so she's a little shy."

"Hi, everyone," I cried. Their good-natured jollity was contagious. I gave Itho a quick squeeze, fur tingling against my bare hip, and handed her to Hibberd. Ziruthine regarded me from large, grave eyes; I leaned over and whispered, "I'd like to see some of your work, if you'd care to show it to me," and was rewarded with a smile. Lior was still in some confusion; I ruffled his hair. "You're right about the skin job. I feel like a puritan. But you see, we tend to wear clothes where I come from."

"I know what clothes are," Trothy cried, looking rather smug. "They're fabric things you put on Outside in the weather." Itho shot her a shocked glance, and she bit her lip. "Well, they used to actually live out in weather all the time where Maggie came from, didn't they?"

My God, I thought, and nodded. "My fabric things seem to be missing."

"Probably the cybs have put them away for when you go back," Hibberd advised me. "Don't worry about Lior —he's just sore he didn't think of plain skin himself."

Trothy clapped her hands twice. "Quiet, everyone. Let's all sit down and give Maggie a chance to get a word in. Then we'll pay our respects to the Daystar and maybe have time for a swim before communion."

We made a circle. I flopped belly down, elbows in the grass, fists under my chin. Itho, cross-legged beside me, innocently dropped her furry little paw on the small of my back and ran her fingers in a circular caress. Physically none of them seemed any older than fourteen or fifteen.

"Kids, I hardly know where to begin. Playing host to time travelers may be daily fare to you, but—"

"Golly no," Trothy said. "You're the first one we've ever heard of. Time transit's something the cyborgs've just invented, I think."

Baffled, I tugged at my lower lip.

"The Daystar told us you're the best known poet of your time and place, Maggie," Ziruthine told me in a soft contralto. "He wishes to honor you."

"Shit!" I struck the turf with my fist. "I've had one

small volume published. Perhaps a thousand people in Australia have heard of me. In fact, I can't even get a bloody job." But an image haunted me: the page of expensive paper, my first poems. Doubtless, though, beings of the awesome resource of Daystar would have no difficulty mocking that up. Why?

Hibberd was laughing. "No, Maggie, you *will* be famous. I mean, you are now, but the Daystar told us you probably haven't even written the works you'll best be remembered for." He trailed off. "If you see what I mean."

"It's crazy," I muttered. "Okay, they'll send me back. But I'll know my own future. I'll be influenced by the poems I haven't written yet. Where did they come from? Maybe I'll just refuse to write them. Christ!"

Furrowed scales: Lior cogitating. "You'll have to ask the Daystar about that. I suppose they'll delete your memory."

In exasperation I cried, "Then what the hell is the point of my being here in the first place?"

"Oh, that's easy. They probably want to map you onto—"

"Hibberd!" Trothy was outraged. "That's the prerogative of the Daystar!"

His copper throat contracted. "Yes. Sorry, Lord." This last seemed to be addressed into the middle distance. He brought his gaze back to meet mine. "The cybs will explain it in due time, Maggie."

In the uncomfortable silence I started to get that locked-in feeling again. It's a trap, I reminded myself, hardly knowing what I meant. Mosaics filled my head, half understood, turning the day's warmth cool in an alchemy of fear: the golden cockerel, Daystar; men in dark oppressive uniforms, murder in their hands; Time broken open like a Technicolor torrent; machines in dreadful colloquy. . . . They're trying to disarm me, and these poor children are just pawns, I thought. Why? Why? Recruit and Assimilate. . . .

Hibberd had risen to his feet, anxiously smiling. "Hey, enough of this serious stuff! Why don't we just show you around, Maggie?"

I nodded and stood up. What I most urgently wanted to investigate was the nature of their hidden masters.

Cybernetic/organism linkages, clearly. But these youngsters were incapable of answering those kinds of questions objectively—that much was also abundantly clear. Trothy took my hand and we started off across the turf toward a pink onion on the other side of the courtyard.

"One thing certainly puzzles me," I said, squinting at fleecy clouds adrift in the flawless summer sky. "What's dirty about weather?"

Nobody said anything for several moments. Trothy blurted, "I'm sorry. I shouldn't have spoken about it. It's just that when you mentioned clothes—"

"But I don't understand why you're apologizing."

"Well, you know." She refused to meet my eyes. "It's not . . . decent . . . to talk about the Outside."

I halted, gesturing helplessly. The sweet wind tossed my hair. "We're outside now! And the weather's perfectly delightful. Why shouldn't—"

Lior guffawed, doubled up in sudden laughter. They all began sniggering and smirking.

"Oh! So that's—"

"She meant—"

"This isn't *weather*, Maggie," Itho got out between smothered giggles. "It's—"

"Hang on, Ith!" Lior jumped up and down in glee. "Let's *show* her. Close your eyes for a moment, Maggie." He focused somewhere beyond the end of his nose. "Set to full moon."

I did not close my eyes.

Brightness drained from the sky.

Even though my mind had leapt ahead, I was not viscerally prepared. My heart contracted, for an instant, in purest superstitious dread.

The sun's fire faded in the darkening heavens, left its orb a silver, pockmarked shield. Stars burst forth in the cloudless night. A dust of diamonds arced the sky: the Milky Way. A cooler breeze dried the sweat that chilled my body for that instant.

"Jesus," I whispered. "It's all an illusion?"

"Well, of course it is, dear," said Itho, rubbing the fur on her short, snub nose. "I mean, I suppose you could look at it that way."

Lior's scales glittered in moonlight; he pressed forward

eagerly, happy as any mariner touting beads and mirrors. "How about Centauri IV, with the crystal mountains? Or Krueger 60, where you get all those weird shadows? Or" —he glanced up at the sun-become-moon—"yeah, Tycho crater, under the Old Dome." His eyes focused once more on the middle distance, and only Hibberd's belated rebuke prevented another monstrous change of scene.

"Stop it, Lior! Maggie isn't used to environment simulation. We're supposed to help her adjust, man." The etched metal of his face, in the flat silver light, reminded me of the primeval mask I'd held in Elfield's laboratory: compassionate, awesome, at once familiar and alien. "Would you like the sun back, Maggie?"

I cleared my throat. "Moonlight's fine, Hibberd." The grassy concourse glimmered emptily between the few exotic structures. Given their total environment control, I wondered why they bothered with buildings at all. The solitude baffled me even more. "Where's everyone else?"

"The Daystar's retinue?" Hibberd shrugged. "Communing, arting, gaming, resting. We're taking you to see some of the others now."

Lights came on in the onion-shaped building as we stepped into its shadow, making it suddenly a fairyland palace.

"Communing?"

"On line with the Daystar and the service net," said Ziruthine, "growing in wisdom."

A vast, complex mural of delicately tinted tiles spiraled the interior bulge of the dome, curving and recurving in hypnotic beauty like mother-of-pearl laid within a conch, to the dizzy spire's glow. Sable, white and gold: the floor was marble, a hundred snakes gorged on their own tails. It was breathtaking. I had part of the answer why they'd preserved architecture.

The youngsters seemed oblivious of magnificence. Their chattering voices echoed, bare feet slapped cool reflections from the walls. I followed them slowly toward the center of the great vacant chamber, abruptly conscious of my aloneness, the taste welling up bitter through my incredulous fascination. . . .

And then, for the first time since I had woken, I realized that I was not necessarily trapped in this meaningless nightmare.

THE JUDAS MANDALA

As one might tongue-probe an aching tooth, my mind reached out for the seething currents of Time and found them, sought purchase, orientation, parallax—

I hurled myself into the torrent...

... and did not move.

"Maggie, what's the *matter*?" Trothy's small anxious face, colors swirling, peered up into mine. I gripped her shoulders, tried again to find that gateway, that shuddering dislocation of space and time which would admit me to Elfield's dawn-bright forest. "Hibberd, Lior, there's something wrong with her!"

I managed a shaky grin. "It's okay. I'm all right now." They clustered about me, at a loss to know what to do. "Really, it's just delayed shock."

I told myself numbly: There's a barrier.

"Perhaps you need more rest," Itho said, her furry hand tentative on my back.

"I'm fine. Let's go on with the tour."

"Well . . ." Trothy was doubtful. I slapped her rump and she grinned. "Come on, then."

A barrier. I shivered, walking with the youngsters into the middle of the chamber. Something dragged me here, I decided, and now It's preventing me from leaving. The cyborgs? That did not seem to fit somehow. The machines which had dredged my mind while I slept had themselves been puzzled, although Daystar had not been surprised when I precipitated into his Byzantine fantasia. Some Entity beyond the cyborgs, manipulating us all? And what of Sriyanie and David? Once more logic failed for lack of data, save for one redoubled resolution: proffer nothing, admit nothing, mistrust everything. It was, to be sure, the counsel of paranoia; it was also, undeniably, the only signpost to survival.

The kids had grouped themselves at five points of a hexagon, directly under the lofty spire, each in the embrace of a self-consuming snake. Trothy broke the pattern to guide me to the sixth point. "Just stand there for a moment, Maggie." She returned to her own position. "Dreamcrib Five."

A purple cylinder of radiance sprang into being about us. My visual field shattered into spinning hypnogogic images. I staggered in dizziness, clapping hands to ears filled with white noise. The sound had deepened immediately to the efficient hum of huge machines; the purple light was gone. We stood in an alcove overlooking a monumental hall crowded with shiny pipe-entwined steel cylinders.

It's another illusion, I told myself. We can't have just—

"Oh, hell," Trothy said. "I'm sorry. I should have warned you. We keep taking things for granted, despite the funny constraints of this language we're using. Transit affects you right down to the quantal level, so there's always a flash of input garbage while your neural indeterminacies are settling back into phase. You sort of don't notice it after the first couple of times."

The others had dispersed toward what looked like an old-fashioned light show, presumably an *nth* century holographic monitor display. I shook my head, rucked my eyebrows up and down once or twice to make sure they were still working.

"Yeah. Where are we now, Trothy?"

"Few hundred kilometers south, I think. These are Dreamtime vats used by most of the humans in the Daystar's domain. You can only see a few thousand here, but there's about fifteen floors of them underneath this one."

"There are *people* in those steel tubes?"

"One in each, on line to the autonomic dream circuits. Bit like the interface we have with the cyborgs during communion, except that the people in the vats aren't on conscious." Her silver mouth quirked with distaste. "They're no good at anything but consuming and breeding, and they'd be pretty damned hopeless at breeding if it wasn't made easy for them."

I thought, suddenly, that I was going to throw up. My legs were numb as I followed her to the monitor. Dear Jesus, I thought. So this is where it ends. Bread & Circus...

"You've got *thirty thousand human beings* laid out there like sides of beef?"

Lior turned from the display, scales mazing its light. His alien features, abruptly macabre, conveyed a technician's complacency.

"A little over fifty thousand," he corrected. He draped his arm over Ziruthine's shoulder. "Dreamcrib Five has a capacity of one hundred thou, but the fertility rate's been dropping despite everything the cyborgs do to encourage reproduction."

"It's the same in all the Domains," said Hibberd. "We're not sure why. It isn't as though they had to wake up, now that pregnancy and parturition can be processed without interrupting dreamtime. Of course, the cyborgs still insist on ethical conscious consent before fertilization, and most of these slobs just can't be bothered after the first time." He sighed. "We may find it necessary to emphasize cloning. It'd be dull if the human species died out through lack of interest."

"I guess it would, at that," I said savagely. Don't hit him. He's as much a victim as they are. "Daystar, you prick," I shouted into the air, "I know you're watching us. It's time we had our little tête-à-tête."

"Oh, Hibby, you're as bad as Lior!" Trothy ran after me, caught me at the entrance to the Transit alcove. There were tears in her eyes. "Maggie, don't be angry—he didn't mean it like that."

I threw her hands off, strode into the Transit locus. "Come on, you tin god. Let's swing that supertechnology into action."

"Maggie, you've got it all wrong. Come back, we want to show you—"

"I've seen all I need to see, Trothy. Take your friends back to the playground." Rage made my voice shake. "God *damn* it, Daystar—"

Violet fire clad me.

My senses fell into ruin and reshaped the world.

I stood in a grimy open square, twilight gray and mournful, broken buildings—crumbled under time's onslaught—reeking of decay, the dead polluted air eddying through the dust like a viscous fluid. There was an alley at my right hand. A young woman, pale, bright garbed and unadorned, crouched over a low marble column. She glanced at me, nodded in satisfaction, took her hand from it.

Dawn touching, obliquely, frost: her hair. That bone and flesh of ivory carved to a black form; that wonder; that astringent flame: her face.

My tense shoulders sagged in relief. And even as I opened my mouth to speak her name, my arms to embrace her, joy staggered at the wrongness, somewhere, everywhere, and she said, "Marguerite Roche, my name is Sriyanie N'Zanvy. Welcome to the Outside."

She had never seen me before in her life.

NINE

Astonishingly, I felt shame in my nakedness.

Sriyanie smiled nervously and offered me the heavy-knit poncho she held. "I'm sorry, Marguerite, I only thought of clothing for you at the last moment. This is rather inadequate, but it should serve until we get inside."

I hesitated, the robe held clumsily in front of me. She was at least five years younger than the last time I had seen her. "No, I'll be okay—"

"Put it on," she said. "Winter's nearly on us and I don't want you to get a chill." Sriyanie started across the filthy cobblestones, then waited for me to follow her. "They still had disease in your time, didn't they?"

I walked beside her, poncho flapping at my thighs. "They did. Yes. They did."

"Press the edges together to seal it. Here, let me help you." Her quick hands stroked the garment, transformed it into a loose tunic. The chill wind still whistled up my bare legs, but I hardly noticed. Her fragrance overwhelmed me. I forced my hands to stay by my sides and followed her across the square. We had made love already in the past, but that was years in the future.

"I was on my way to see Daystar," I managed. "Won't he be a trifle tetchy?"

Sriyanie smiled. Her nervousness was almost gone. "He doesn't know. We're phasing at random into virtual time sequences. The vertical component is less than a nanosecond. Our entropy gradient's been diverted, so to speak, at ninety degrees to the mainstream continuity."

"Remarkable," I said, stubbing my toe on a jutting stone. "Sriyanie, I don't have the faintest idea what you're talking about."

"Never mind," she said. "I'll explain it properly when we get to the Sanctuary. Roughly, the rest of the universe is at a standstill until we decide to climb back on. The Daystar doesn't know you're here, because as far as the main sequence is concerned you're still in transit."

"Mmm," I said. "So much for cause and effect. How come we can see and hear each other, not to mention the slight risk of asphyxiation?"

She shot me a startled glance. "Marguerite, my field is Mid-English linguistics—the math is beyond both of us. Basically, we're the only dysentropic probability vector in these 'virtual realities.' The ontology's plastic. There's a sort of consensual cocoon around us, modifying our immediate environment synchronistically. I'll introduce you to a specialist one day."

There wasn't much I could say to that. We entered what once must have been a major thoroughfare. Dust caked the smashed footpaths. A few hardy weeds thrust tentatively through fissures in the pitted concrete, lost and bewildered, perhaps, by nature's betrayal. "Sanctuary. Hmm. Your headquarters?"

Puzzled. "Head—? Marguerite, we're a functional anarchy, not a wired-up hive—"

I touched her arm, and the shock almost made me stumble. My God, I thought, am I in *love* with this woman?

"Yeah, Sriyanie, fine. I'm not enraptured by bullshit patristic hierarchies myself. Still, communications is the core of any rebellion. I mean, I guess Sanctuary must be a clearinghouse, right?"

Her fingers danced a tattoo together. "Marguerite, your terminology's inappropriate. Those of us who live Outside couldn't conceivably mount rebellion against the cybs.

THE JUDAS MANDALA

We're not insurgents—just staying alive and free is almost more than we can manage. If the cyborgs didn't provide us with food and materials—"

"The *cyborgs?*" I stopped, appalled. "You mean you're just one more crew of parasites on those bastards?"

Stingingly, then, across the mouth, she struck me. My fingers splayed automatically; I seized her hand in defensive anger. The outrage in her eyes made me let it fall.

"You arrogant fool! You know nothing, *nothing*, of . . . Eight people risked the freedom of their souls to get you out of that place today, despite the fact that you botched it up, and you—" At the verge of tears she stopped, put about herself a cloak of icy grace. "I forget myself, Marguerite. You lack an understanding of this world's complexity, and I was wrong to be offended by words spoken in ignorance."

"Sriyanie, I'm sorry. I've been thrown from one insanity to another so fast I—"

"Of course. And I apologize for striking you." Coldly, she turned away. "Now let us proceed to the Sanctuary."

I moved so instinctively I hardly knew what was happening. She fell against my breast like a discarded wooden puppet, stiff and unbending even where rusty joints are hinged, and I tightened my arms until the edge of her jaw was a pain in my breastbone, the flowers of her white hair in my face and my mouth against her cold small ear hot with self-reproach, burgeoning tenderness growing to a white flame in me, telling myself: I *cannot* tell her the truth of the past; Time is a circle that I dare not breach until my ignorance, indeed, is filled with an understanding of that circle; holding her against me until her outrage should find voice or thaw; and the edges and tensions of her body turned then to soft flesh, and we cradled one another in the chill, filthy breeze.

She stood back from me, at last, sniffing, wiping at her wet eyes with her wrist, and smiled ruefully.

" 'I grow too fast,' " she said.

I grinned back at her, tugging like that adolescent at my long hair. " '. . . And frequently lay foot on poisoned weeds.' I guess I haven't really changed much since I was thirteen, petal. And please call me Maggie." We started along the broken street again, arms linked. "Hey, how the hell *did* anyone get hold of that poem? I burned it when I was a kid."

"They got it from you." She conjured a small book from a pocket. I'd seen a page from that book before: a freaky feeling. "You'll dictate it under hypnoprobe for the New Oxford Multiversity collected edition." Her teeth closed with an audible snap and she put the volume away. "My faux pas. Forget I said that, Maggie. I'm not supposed to talk about anything you haven't lived through yet."

That protocol made me feel slightly easier about my selective candor with her. But I said, "That's been puzzling me. You know I was on a conducted tour of the controlled environment?"

She nodded. "Ziruthine has sympathies with the Free people. She's been synchronous ever since her Nest was chosen to take you through the Domain."

That raised more questions than it settled; I let it pass. "One of the kids hinted that I'm to be sent back to the twentieth century with my brain, uh, laundered. It sounds logical—I can't imagine any other way to keep me clear of causal loops. But, Sriyanie, I know the cybs are prepared to kill me if they can. Surely that would short-circuit their own past?"

"They wouldn't dare!" she cried vehemently. "They can't be that reckless—"

"Petal, they've tried twice already. I can't guess why they want to. If I'm so insignificant that they can expunge my time line without lousing up their own history, why bother to do it in the first place?"

"Insignificant?" She made a noise that was not a laugh. "Hardly that, Maggie. It's true there're millions in any era who could be abolished without raising a significant causal ripple on the main sequence—but you're not one of them."

She turned toward a long ugly warehouse fronting the street on our right. It was slightly better preserved than most of the buildings we'd passed. We went into the darkness of the loading bay, paused before the corroded entrance. Sriyanie spoke her name, and the slab of gritty concrete we stood on sank slowly into the ground. A strip of warm apricot edged the slab, grew, became an extensive, cheerily illuminated room. As soon as we stepped

THE JUDAS MANDALA

into the room, tracking gray dust across the maroon carpet, the slab rose to slot once more into the loading bay floor.

"Make yourself comfortable." The girl indicated several luxurious, brightly colored couches. She lifted her palms to her face, rubbed warmth into her pale cheeks. "Are you hungry? I'll have some refreshments sent in. And I'll fetch some garments—or you can go naked if you prefer. We usually skin down when we're indoors . . . but I seem to recall that your epoch suffered a nudity taboo."

"When in Rome," I muttered. "I'm learning to adjust."

I tugged the poncho over my head and handed it to her —and then felt a flash of injured egotism when she failed to react in the slightest. She slipped gracefully out of her yellow two-piece hugsuit, then confounded me by leaning over and darting her tongue into my ear, dancing away with her bundle of clothes as I instantly reached up to her.

"Not now, Maggie. We've got a lot to discuss before you go back to the Daystar, and I can't sustain Timestop indefinitely. Service," she added, "a pot of hot coffee for two and a plate of high-protein croissants." She looked pleased with herself at getting it right.

Watching her, I remembered with a pang my suspicious desire for her body, in my past, her future. Time was an ocean of paradox and I rode its strange violence like a demented sailor hurricane swept from the spurious safety of his ship. I shivered. "There are power limitations to your equipment?"

"Equipment?" Sriyanie cocked her head to one side, gold-pale eyebrows drawn together.

"Whatever it is you use to keep us here."

"Oh!" She laughed in surprise. "There's no equipment, Maggie. The only mechanism I've used was the Transit discontinuity. Timestop's purely an organic function. I'm doing it all on my own, with a little help from your DNA."

A melodic chord sang and our snack glided across the room on an invisible beam. Sriyanie took the tray, positioned it in midair between us, poured steaming coffee into white, translucent bowls. I leaned forward to accept one; fingers trembling, I blew across the rich liquid and stared at the young woman. "So the cyborgs," I said carefully, "lack this capability."

"We think so." She bit delicately into a pastry. "Most of them have dispensed with any organic components at all. An organic nervous system can be supported and amplified by aninertia and perfect nutrients and enzyme regulation and cybernated extensions, but it *still* wears out after a couple of thousand years. The original cyborgs eventually had their neural constellations mapped onto energy matrices which can't deteriorate. The initiates usually opt for the same process as soon as they're accepted—and even the few who've retained their human brains seem to have lost the peculiar holistic characteristics which are involved in time manipulation."

"My God. So it wasn't Daystar who brought me here from the twentieth century."

Sriyanie put her bowl down and regarded me somberly.

"Maggie, that's precisely why you're so important. You did it alone. You moved yourself four thousand years up the main sequence. Neither we nor the cybs know of any other conscious entity in history with that ability."

"No one else has jumped so far? But that still doesn't explain—"

"I expressed myself poorly. Maggie, what you did was *totally* unique. Time transit has always been a theoretical possibility—but you're the only person in known history who's ever done it."

"But Sri, this limbo, this Timestop condition we're in . . ." I swung my arm wide.

"It's the sole form of temporal control we've been able to attain . . . and the least significant of all the theoretical variants. Timestop lets us talk to each other without surveillance, which is undeniably useful, but its principal use is metaphysical. Our numbers are too few and our resources too limited for guerrilla warfare. Understand, we're faced by a coalition of cybernetic intelligences extending beyond the solar system. With genuine time transit, though . . ." Her tone became exultant. "It's a wild factor, unaccountable, immensely potent. Can you see now why they have to stop you?"

"Uh-huh." But she was wrong. At best her truth constituted no more than a fragment of the mosaic. I stretched back into the relaxer, hands on my lap. "Sriyanie, your intelligence people are slipping. I am *not* the only one with time motility. They tried to kill me while I was still in my own century."

Her hand flew to her mouth. "That's impossible! Time transit *can't* be mechanized. If the cybs had somehow learned to train hivers to do it, Ziruthine or someone would have told us."

"Sriyanie, there's another possibility. If I *am* the only human so far with time motility, the assassins must be from your own future." Again, some intuition restrained me from telling her about the loop which eventually would take her into my past. But I added dourly, "In fact, if time jumping is a transmissible skill, history must be crawling with time travelers who haven't been born yet."

She worried her knuckles with small, perfect teeth.

"I don't think so. Time is not that simple. Any mathematical model which permits transit up and down the main sequence must start by rejecting lineality, or it breaks down under the weight of cumulative singularities. But you're right about the assassins. They're obviously from farther up the sequence. Maggie, that's terrifying."

"You keep citing theoretical models, Sriyanie. Surely you'd considered that the cybs might eventually learn how to manipulate time, even if they have to use human agents."

"Maggie, you don't appreciate how stunned we were when you suddenly arrived out of the past. Time transit has never really been more than a remote, unproven extension of Timestop. There's been sophisticated speculation ever since Elfield's seminal studies way back in your own century, but the gap between theory and practice has never been bridged. Until now. Until you. Everything's happened so quickly we haven't had time to work out the implications properly."

I didn't dare let myself think about that Elfield loop. Guarding my face, I thought instead: They're like second-generation chiliasts, their faith betrayed into unthinking dogma by an uneventful turn of the millennium. The analogy was unjust, but relevant: for who is more surprised than the ritualist when apocalypse explodes outside his window? That train of thought led straight to an unwelcome corollary; I grimaced.

"I'm nobody's Joan of Arc, honey. There's a stink in my nostrils, but don't expect me to march in front of any banners. Okay, I'm a biological freak. I can do unlikely things with time. But that's my genes, baby, not my head. I'm just a quiet out-of-work nihilist—"

The mildness of her tone cut me down, where hysterical fervor would merely have encouraged me. "It's too late to quit, Maggie. Resent it or not, you were committed from the moment the cyborgs learned you could move in time. Control is their obsession, their very essence. Now they know time transit is possible, they'll master it even if it takes ten thousand years—and then they'll seek you out and destroy you, because you represent the only threat they've ever faced."

She did not have to add that it certainly would be that way because, in a sense, that was already the way it had been, in their future; where else *could* my would-be murderers have come from? Sriyanie's group itself? My God. Paranoia. I could not believe it. With numb fingers I pressed my aching temples, overwhelmed by futility and despair. Someone had twice failed to kill me; I could not wait passively for them to try again. Time's cyclopean presence bent down, dense, opaque, unyielding, to suffocate my spirit. What would be had been. How might I defeat an enemy when my every gambit was, to him, a matter of historic record?

And yet: paradox. . . . If I were known to this world for poems I had not yet written, could I be killed before I wrote them? Time, Sriyanie had said, is not that simple. But if it were not, if Time twisted loops within its tesseract, perhaps my fate was not inevitable.

I glanced at her. She regarded me with patient silence. With a blinding shock, my exhausted mind found the datum it had lost in the turmoil of my first tiny jumps through time.

Sitting on her silken bed in Elfield's mansion I had moved back in time, *and I had not encountered my prior self!*

Somehow, I had displaced that earlier Maggie, made her . . . redundant. Unnecessary. I had recapitulated my presence on the main sequence, carrying full memory with me, and abolished my earlier presence.

"Dear Christ!" I closed my eyes and slumped back in the relaxer.

It had not occurred in the square, when I had helped myself escape the cyborgs' gunmen. Okay, the laws of temporal transposition are complex, holistic, permitting at least two radically variant phenomena. But under some circumstances *events could be altered retroactively*. I sat up again, tense with excitement.

"All right, Sriyanie. I'm confused, but I think we may be able to beat them. By God, we're not lost yet."

She pushed aside the floating tray, stooped to clutch my hand. "We'll do everything we can to back you up. You're vulnerable, Marguerite, but you have an incalculable advantage so long as you are the only one with full time control. They can attack you from the future, but that future is contingent on the present. If our theoreticians are correct, you may be able to alter the vector of the main sequence, at least up to the point when the cyborgs develop their own time-traveling agents."

Her confirmation of my own analysis had an unexpected effect: another anomaly struck me, and my elation vanished in a prickling of cold sweat.

"Just a moment, Sriyanie. Let's assume the murder attempts will be initiated by the cyborgs in the future. Okay. I didn't die, so they'll fail. There's no crucial causal loop there, even though it makes my head spin to picture it." And what of the part her future self would play? I pushed the question aside. "But there *has* been a loop created already. How did Daystar know who I was when I first appeared unless he'd got a warning from his own future?"

Her head jerked back, eyes wide. "He was *expecting* you?"

"You didn't realize that? He knew me, addressed me by name. How could he have known without being told?"

The young woman stood up, her face blank.

"It certainly complicates matters. It's like moving through fog, Maggie. If the cyborgs were confident of their hold on the main sequence, why didn't they kill you when you first appeared? I'm sorry. That's a dreadfully insensitive thing to say. But we *have* to think this out coldly. If they'll be able to send back warning of your impending arrival, why can't they also communicate the technique? Obviously they will *not* do so or the Daystar would not need you now."

She shook her head in perplexity and a tiny sound emerged from her throat. "Maggie, if only one of our temporal theorists had been here! We'd planned to have Ziruthine bring you in later, when we were better prepared."

"And I blew it by shouting at Daystar."

"You didn't know, Maggie. But it didn't leave me much choice—I *had* to intercept you. I was the only synchronous linguist near a Transit locus. If you'd faced him in ignorance you'd have been brainscrubbed. But I've been so little help—"

"Sweetheart, that isn't true!" I drew her down beside me, and my flesh tingled where hers met mine at shoulder, hip, thigh; the hairs of my arm strained toward her. An odd blend of lust and tenderness colored the dread which was moving in slow, murky waves through me. "We've outstripped theory. I doubt that any of your experts could make better sense of this farrago than we have. Besides," I said, grinning, and tightened my arm around her, "I'm sure none of the experts is nearly as pretty as you."

The tensions in her muscles eased and she made a sound suspiciously like a derisive snort, grinning back at me. "That sort of flattery's archaic, Maggie. *Everybody's* pretty now, even the experts—genetic cosmetics saw to that a few thousand years ago. The thing that makes *you* so fascinating is, uh, what the old books used to refer to as 'character.'"

"Thanks a lot, kid."

Her warmth flooded me. I pulled her down alongside me on the glowing fabric of the couch, and the scent of her juices came to me. My own hard-knotted angst transmuted to a zestful, hungry joy: flame, wind, roses. Sriyanie wrapped her limbs around mine with equal eagerness. We devoured one another with ferocious greed. It was a purge, as much as anything, for our dread.

It is no accident that *power* connotes both energy and executive ascendancy. Nor is it unrealistic, as Marx and his followers argued, to see history as a halting dialectic between the radical imperatives of technology and the internecine rivalries of its human inventors. Had not the cyborgs long since attained effortless dominion over the postindustrial processes of communication, production, and transportation, the development of Transit would have sundered the stability of human society. In the event, it was no more than an addendum to their total control.

Or so it seemed. The dialectic, in fact, had merely gone underground. For Transit discontinuity opened the door to Timestop, to ontological vistas so dramatic that no element of the puritan oppositional society was unshaken. If the Frees had hesitated at the entrance to a blighted utopia—relieved, after all, of onerous drudgery, of disease, of unnecessary ignorance: all the equivocal gratuities of their cyborg potentates—Timestop hurled them into authentic anarchy.

A concentration camp, however lavishly appointed, thrives on a social contract of discipline and hierarchy. Timestop was a condition of experience utterly outside the parameters of the cyborg reality. It shattered the possibility of hierarchy in a single blow. Autonomy was no longer a marginal dream; it became the fundamental defining condition of Free existence.

I cannot explain Timestop to you, any more than I could detail the technology of Transit discontinuity. The science of our textbooks is still scratching at the edges of an adequate geometrodynamic. The closest we come to discontinuity theory is our poor grasp of the physics of black hole singularities. Nor (at this moment) would I do so if I could. I am not irresponsible. The consequences of importing detailed insights from one era to a previous one are still grossly uncertain. Let others venture upon the hazards and morality of that step.

Even so, the broadest outlines are feasible. Timestop operates in an infinitesimal gap, perhaps the duration of an electron's leap across the Forbidden Region between one energy level and the next (though the physics of that proposition are doubtless as erroneous as Aristotle's)—too brief, at any rate, to be observed even by the cyborgs' magnificently augmented senses. Do you see why Sanctuary and other handsome drop-in centers like it around the globe could not be venues where the delegates of oppositional groups might meet in null-time conspiracy, debate, or horse-trading? How could they occasion the exquisite timing necessary? For they would all be required to enter the Transit discontinuity at exactly the same instant. To do otherwise, by even one further bounce of the electron, would partition them in isolated universes.

Timestop, not Transit, created the world's first genuine anarchic community. As Sriyanie explained all this to me —with the greatest difficulty, for I could hardly encompass such new perspectives with any ease—I understood why she had been puzzled by my suggestion that Sanctuary was HQ to a Resistance movement. For Timestop, by its nature, could serve little tactical, oppositional function. It was, rather, the arena for an elevation of consciousness, a heuristic for the discovery that the world is neither illusory Maya nor insistent Fact but something more transcendent and intimate than either.

"I wonder . . . Sriyanie, what you're saying rings a lot of bells. The disruption of time, the merging of minds . . . Is it possible that Timestop has been discovered before, without the technology of Transit?"

She sat forward. "Almost certainly, Maggie. But it's been lost again, over and over. There are a few hints in myth." She raised her voice slightly. "Can we hear that quote from the Christian Apocrypha?"

"Certainly, Sriyanie," a fine, resonant voice said from the air. I jumped. Sri smiled, and touched my arm. "I'm sorry," she said. "It's just an information retrieval system. Go on."

The voice had been keyed to English; it alarmed me somewhat that the thing clearly had been listening to our discussion. I told myself that it was merely a mechanism. Hard to believe as the rich tones, beautiful as Olivier's, said, "The passage is from the Protevangelion and relates to Joseph's brief epiphany as he sought a midwife for his semidivine spouse, Mary. 'As I was going,' Joseph states, 'I looked up into the air, and I saw the clouds astonished, and the fowls of the air stopping in the midst of their flight. And I looked toward the earth and saw a table spread and working people sitting around it, but their hands were upon the table, and they did not move to eat. . . . And I beheld sheep dispersed, and yet the sheep stood still. And the shepherd lifted up his hand to smite them, and his hand continued up. And I looked unto a river and saw the kids with their mouths close to the water and touching it, but they did not drink.'

"It is the prevailing opinion of the Eighth Level theoreticians," added the machine, "that this fragment, though embedded in myth, recalls a genuine achronic event. Lacking the techniques of discontinuity, the unknown illuminatus was not able to extend his consciousness into sustained orthogonal duration."

"Thank you," Sriyanie said. "Plenty of other unreliable records suggest pre-Transit achronia," she told me, "but they're of interest only to antiquarians. None of them plausibly indicates the capacity to do what you've done—transit *through* time, rather than halt it or move sideways."

It took nearly four hours of intense obscure circling, reiteration, definition, and elaboration before my overloaded mind was even halfway to understanding the nature of Sriyanie's world. From time to time, in the midst of earnest exposition, Sri lapsed into mathematical notation, a crystalline hexadecimal language devised centuries after my era. The paradox was infuriating: I lacked many of the elementary conceptual skills she took for granted, yet she dared not employ direct Ontological Recapitulation to brief me, for fear that the Daystar would crack my mind like a lobster's shell and tear out that most sacrosanct of secrets. In retrospect, perhaps that calculation seems insane; if the cyborgs could do that, they would almost certainly penetrate *my* stupendous faculty—and if they had mine, Timestop was a bagatelle. But Sri's logic skidded in the face of years of stringent conditioned ritual.

"We can use a paragnostic block to protect what I'm telling you now," she said. "Full Recapitulation employs a whole battery of them, at the deep structure level, but you're not ready for that yet. Forgive me, Maggie, but in this respect you're like a child of the First Level. Merging would be incomplete. The gaps would show, and the Daystar would rip your defences to shreds."

I shook my head blindly. "Sriyanie, your entire relationship with the cyborgs baffles me entirely. Look, you said Ziruthine told you what I was doing while she and

I were still in the domain. How the hell did she manage that without the machines detecting her message?"

She sighed wearily and poured us each another bowl of coffee. "Let's go back to the beginning, Maggie. You have to realize that the world is not made the way your era thought it was. Underlying the obvious cause-and-effect reality there's the great web of synchronicity. Everything is linked by affinity. Events occur confluentially, without the crude kind of causality which is involved in the physics of exchange forces."

With abrupt, shocked incredulity, I said, "You mean magic. The Laws of Similarity and Contagion." I laughed.

"No," she said patiently. "The magic archetype is just as faulty as the causality model. Both hint at the truth—neither is anywhere near it. Leave it at this: while you were in the Dreamvat area, it was my turn to rest in synchrony with Ziruthine's perceptions. Call it empathy, if you like, or telepathy, though it's *not* that. I was not reading her mind, but I was, on a simple level, co-experiencing her reality. When it became obvious what your intentions were, I had to intercept you. Being in synchrony, I was able to activate my Transit locus at the same instant the Daystar pulled *you* on to the discontinuity."

I got to my feet and beat my fists against my scalp. "But I thought it's impossible to arrange simultaneous entry to Transit without physical proximity!"

Softly, taking my hand, she said, "Not impossible, but very difficult. Sustaining synchrony with more than one or two people at once would be impossible."

The old town square, she added, was one of many "sacred places" the Frees had built into their elaborate rituals. She'd had to enter the discontinuity in order to intercept me. Her specified Transit destination was the decayed square—the scene, hundreds of years before, of some convenient notable enterprise.

When I was ready to be sent on to complete my instantaneous journey to Daystar, she would release her hold on Timestop and emerge, in fact, where we'd met several hours "earlier": at the ancient locus in the square. There, for the benefit of any monitoring cybs, she'd pursue a meaningless series of apparently superstitious observances before returning through Transit to Sanctuary.

THE JUDAS MANDALA

I brooded on that for a while. It seemed preposterous, until it came to me that most rituals accrete around the kernels of their predecessors, as Christian and Muslim churches were built where possible on the ruins of pagan temples. In this case the rituals had been devised almost cold-bloodedly for cosmetic purposes, but the principle was similar.

"Clark Kent operated under much the same rubric," I muttered.

"I'm sorry?"

"Mythological reference. Sri, shouldn't you have chosen a more secluded spot than the middle of a town square, rancid as it is?"

"One Transit locus is as good as another. Besides—" she lowered her eyes—"with interception off the discontinuity, there's a small chance that the locus will blow."

I winced. "Which'd be pretty messy in a closed room. Hmmm. Well, what do we do now?"

"Maggie, we've established synchrony with one another. As soon as I get back here, in real time, I'll start a serial conference with everyone in the local Free community. We've never had an emergency like this before, but the procedures are all mapped out."

It amounted to this: Sri would take several people into Timestop with her, communicating in total detail through Ontological Recap. They in turn would vector the news out to others and those to others still. There was an appreciable risk that all this sudden cascading motion would alert the monitoring cyborgs, but it was a risk which had to be taken. The Free people, no less than I, were at a crossroads.

The paragnostic block involved machines I never saw, fields massaging my neural tissues in ways subtle beyond comprehension. When it was done I felt no different. I probed again for the Something, for the Entity which apparently had brought me here, and found nothing to give me comfort. Incomprehensible facts swirled in my mind. All my verities were blown tattered in this gale. I began to feel truly terrified.

It was not necessary to walk back to the scene of interception, but we did it anyway. Nor was it essential that this invented universe retain its apparent identity with the bleak, polluted horror of real time, but Sri kept it that way. The protocols of Timestop were utterly conservative, by choice; if it were not for a ruthless habit of consensus, the infinitely plastic void would lure the human mind into madness.

The desolate gray sky hung like Doomsday evening, trapped in the pseudomovement of its timeless instant. We crossed the square, and I pulled the borrowed poncho off over my head. I considered what Sriyanie had mentioned about the hazards of interception and wasn't sure that annihilation by Transit malfunction might not be preferable to what I would shortly confront.

My stomach crawled. There was something unutterably disgusting about the cyborg Domain, beyond the immediate threat it represented for me, beyond even the loathsomeness of what had been done to the human race. A stink of corruption filled the cyborgs' sanitized air. I shivered, overwhelmed with a dark awareness of those ancient, fleshless, inturned intellects; I remembered their probing caress, the passionless vaults of their icy minds.

Sriyanie took the discarded garment, hugged me. We kissed one another gently. The confidence she radiated would have been more encouraging if my thoughts hadn't kept returning to the barrier which had thwarted me in the Transit dome. Sriyanie knew nothing of this. It pained me to keep so much of what I knew from her, but the knowledge of that loop from her future to my past was too ambivalent. Besides, if the barrier continued to block me I was lost anyway. I bowed sardonically in the direction of the steadfast shade of Norman Vincent Peale—most of my earliest reading matter had come from a huge moldering pile of *Reader's Digest*s stacked in my grandfather's toolshed.

"Hey, honey, it's cold out here. If Daystar sees me covered in goose bumps he'll wonder where I've been."

"You won't be," she reminded me. "Entry and exit from Ur-Time is probabilistic. It's a function of total context. Except for your memory acids, you'll come out of it in the same physical configuration as you went in. If it were otherwise, the Lords would have learned about Timestop long ago."

I was instantly sober. The horror I'd been trying to quell

inundated me. "You have a wonderful way with words, linguist."

"I know." She placed a final kiss between my naked breasts. "May your anger be arms and armor enough to rout him." And she went across the broken, filthy cobblestones, head proudly high, to the ancient Transit locus.

I stared at the arctic sky and let rage flood me.

TEN

Releasing Maggie to the tugging tensions of her discontinuity vector, watching her vanish like an imploding bubble, Sriyanie is assailed by loss and fear. The emotion startles her; she is appalled by its intensity. Her self-control staggers. For a moment she leans on the grimy, cracked marble pillar which houses the partonic circuits of the locus, and her muscles tremor. What has this hard, fierce woman done to her? She has not been so vulnerable to the anguish of sudden love since that day the cyborg Lord stalked into the Blue Torus and ripped her from her Five.

A moment longer she holds herself in Timestop, seeking calmness. She interrogates, autonomically, the subliminal bond which represents her synchrony with Maggie, and new shock sweeps her. The pulse of pseudoidentity is doubled: beyond the merged harmony of her deepest cycles and those of Marguerite Roche is a further harmonic she has never sensed before. It is a man. His dark, powerful pulse links with her and Maggie in a whining web, taut and singing. And beyond the triptych, Something looms, greater still in magnitude and significance. . . .

She gasps, and the intuition is lost. The extended identity field has enclosed itself within her. Warily, filled with suspicions she cannot name, Sriyanie withdraws into passive attentiveness and allows herself to slip out of orthogonal time into the mainstream reality.

The sky contracts into darkness.

There is an instant of total, stunning confusion. Her pupils dilate. A violet tractor beam scores the sky, bearing a neural disruptor at its focus, dropping, as she watches, in a terrible purposive swoop toward the old markets. Cold wind, a night breeze off the dead ocean, catches her hair; the air's stench is foul. The poncho falls unnoticed to the ground. Her mind accelerates, holding thought in abeyance, delegated totally to perception. Almost at her feet a man groans. High above, a pinpoint of brightness flares; she drops her newly adjusted gaze lest the light dazzle her and sees that the man's nose is shattered, his face covered in blood.

All of this is impossible, she knows. She has gone into Transit in daylight and emerged at night. There is no reason for these Nest humans to be stationed in the square unless the cyborgs have monitored her in Timestop and sent them here in ambush. This is doubly absurd: the running men are not aware of her, are not looking for her. Analysis comes to her in a gestalt, a single recognition. It includes the fact that the maimed human before her is a Nest technician, clad in the heavy garments worn by those few hivers obliged to venture beyond the simulations into the Outside.

There is a shout from the far side of the square. Her presence has been observed at last. A hiver is leaning forward bent-legged in the gloom, raising an energy weapon. Sriyanie's hand is already on the locus plate, transmitting the code for Suva, a survival routine implanted during her very first Transit with Beth. The discontinuity activates as a searing bolt lashes past her face, as the hiver alters his aim the fraction necessary to incinerate her—

—And she hurls herself into the safety of Timestop. There is no reprieve from shock. Before she can take a breath in the pale dawn light of pseudo-Suva, Sriyanie sees the familiar face regarding her with relief, sees the woman's arms come up to embrace her, sees Beth here in Timestop with her.

"Sri! Little one!" Astonishingly, as she finds herself falling against the other's breast, she realizes that Beth is weeping. Clumsily they let themselves down onto the cold sand, clutching one another, and Sriyanie gives up the struggle for poise.

Eventually, when they have regained themselves, Beth says, "You've been gone five days."

Incredulously: "Gone? Something happened, Beth, but—I've been in Sanctuary. When I came out of Ur-Time the square was full of Nest techs. It was *dark,* Beth. Natural night! I came back on the main sequence *hours* later than I left it." A beat. "Oh."

"Days, Sri," Beth repeats softly. "You disappeared completely. The woman from the past came back and now she's gone. The Lords have been looking for you, Sri. They couldn't find you. We thought you were dead too, little one. We thought they'd killed you. Then we found they were searching for *you.*"

Urgently, unheeding, Sriyanie says, "They've killed Maggie?" Nightmare. "Did you say Maggie's dead?" It numbs her; she feels nauseated.

"The woman betrayed you. She betrayed us all."

Shrilly, fingers digging into her Friend's arm, she cries, "Is she *dead?*"

Beth's face is like a mask, like a Bugaku mask in the faint, greenish dawn. She stares out at the dull waves thudding in to shore. "I hope so."

Sriyanie is silent. Obviously that is not what Beth said. Eyes stinging, she toys without knowing it with a strand of long white hair. Her throat aches. Too much has occurred too abruptly. She climbs to her feet and stumbles away along the beach. After a moment, the older woman stands up and follows her.

"We refused to give up hope," Beth says at her shoulder. "The woman had demonstrated that time transit is feasible. We set up a crash experimental program, serial conferencing in Timestop. We're on the edge of it, Sri. It's a talent, but we think it can be trained. Evoked. As she did with you." There is a ghastly edge to her tone. After a time she says, more wearily, "I brought the Four of your Five to the Fiji redoubt and set up an interception roster. You came back into synchrony a few real-time seconds ago, but we missed you. Then you vectored to Suva and I had a chance to grab you off the discontinuity."

Sriyanie halts and places her cold hand on Beth's cheek.

For the first time she notices the exhaustion in the woman's eyes.

"Thank you, Ummy." It cannot have been easy for them. The implications slowly filter through her fatigue. Frightened, then, she asks, "But what can I do, Beth? I have to leave Timestop eventually. They won't miss me a second time."

Beth is grave. "You still haven't understood, Sri." The tendons at her throat quiver under tension. "You jumped up the main sequence! Child, you moved yourself through time. If you could do it once, you can do it again. And so can we." With passion, Beth says, "We have to stop her. Go back and stop her before any of this ever happened. Wipe it out. Or everything we've ever lived for has been for nothing."

The proposition, the perspective, leaves Sriyanie aghast. She cannot recognize her loving Other. Nor can she recall having willed her flight through time. If five days have been obliterated, if she has skipped through the n-space manifold, there was no element of intention in the act. It is instinct which has driven her from one danger to another, and then to its avoidance. It is as Maggie has told her: time travel is something done with the entrails, the inarticulate inner workings of the body and mind. Little wonder the cyborgs cannot locate its key.

She quails. The contact of her hand in Beth's breaks. It has been her intention to meld in Ontological Recapitulation with her Other; now the trust, the requisite harmony, has gone. Sriyanie rises and faces the sea. She reaches within herself for some inkling of time's path.

The world fades utterly; Beth is gone; Something vast and incomparably powerful takes her into Its charge and plunges her without hesitation to a vortex of motion she cannot command,

falls through centuries down the great cliff face of Time, plunging like a toy caught in a torrent, the web of extended identity tightening on her, the Being looming like a god, some fantastic affinity drawing her toward the dark man whose faceless image she had found in the echoing cavern of her conjoined being-in-Maggie

and she's blinking amid low cityscape, under a night sky unbefouled by the stench and fumes of poisoned millennia, an archaic vehicle zooming away from her on a long, straight road and a young man stalking angrily up steps to enter a hideous building, his back to her as she stands on rubbery legs; poles strung with wires, yellow tubes of light buzzing with insects in the heavy heat; squalid terraces, glazed windows, wooden doors with peeling paint, yet *alive*—

She is no longer in Timestop, nor has she passed to real-time Suva as her trajectory had ordained. Swaying, refusing to faint, hands to her cold face, she knows that she is not, indeed, any longer in her own world. Like Maggie, like the tough, fierce woman from history, she has been cast through time. She has been plucked from Timestop and thrown four thousand years into antiquity.

Another vehicle approaches, blocky, suspended on wheels, driven—if its ugly noise is any guide—by an internal combustion engine. Fossil fuel. That localizes the period still more: she is somewhere between the second and, at most, the last decade of the twentieth century. The machine fails to strike her, by a more than adequate margin, but she shies at its rush of air, the protracted blast of its horn.

Light flickers, smears the spherical entrance which swallowed the young man. No one else is in sight. Sriyanie hesitates, moves on trembling legs to the steps. Her own volition has not brought her to this place and time. It has been wrought by something outside her science and, apparently, her time. She tells herself: Maggie is dead.

Numbly, she enters the building. Harsh artificial light shines off tatters and streamers of torn plastic, great bags and tubes subsiding from metal struts. One arm encounters some soft, squashy surface. Across the large irregular room the lean youth is ripping the curious plastic appointments to shreds.

Sriyanie watches this activity blankly, adrift, without reference points, seeing only the man's anger and determination. His anger frightens her. Without warning, a new perception explodes into her mind: this is the man whose alien harmonic has overplaid the synchrony linking her with Maggie. She takes a step toward him and once more tells herself: Maggie is dead. Yet time has been bent. Perhaps, for Maggie, none of this has happened yet. Involuntarily, with dread and hope, she cries out.

The youth whirls from his ferocious work. "What the hell are you doing here?"

Sriyanie draws back. He is speaking Mid-English. His bearded blade face has hardly firmed from adolescence, his eyes are sullen and almost childishly petulant. He steps toward her, frowning. "Who are you?" he cries. "My God, you haven't been lurking in here all along, have you?" His cheeks darken still more, and his right arm twitches up defensively across his body.

In the youth's stance and emotional indices Sriyanie discerns that his destructive rioting can serve no legitimate purpose, that he stands now at a pivot. Is this why I've been put here? she asks herself. Composure returns.

"My name is Sriyanie N'Zanvy," she tells him in a placatory tone. To her left, behind a huge, deflating tube, the iris door is still open to the hot, stifling street beyond. Gesturing, she tells him, "The entrance was open. I wondered what all the noise was." She touches an orange plastic bubble, keeping her eyes on him. "You're dissatisfied with the way this is?"

"Jesus. You guessed." He is truculent, but his fury is ebbing to scorn. "I can just tell that you have a mind like a steel trap. It must be my night for beautiful women." He hesitates, and his quick words fail in some interior confusion. Turning, he stares at the mess he's made and shrugs. "What the hell. I don't approve of gross displacement activities anyway."

Sriyanie circles him, getting the feel of the place, sensing his injured, proprietorial feelings. "A woman?"

He looks at her sharply. "You saw her drive off?"

"No. I don't think so. But you said—"

He shrugs again. "Yeah. A woman. Big deal. So much for the cathartic function of art."

"*You* made this place?" It intrigues her; it is immature, like the youth, but its bold use of archetypes appeals to her. I am in the ancient past, she tells herself, awash with the wonder of it. Beneath the wonder is her baffled grief: Maggie is dead. Sriyanie forces her attention to the moment, to the damaged structure. Clearly it is intended to be in motion, to constitute a mythic framework.

"My design," he tells her. Is he disappointed that she doesn't know already? "Look, I think you'd better leave now. I'm not in a very convivial mood." He walks past

THE JUDAS MANDALA

the slashed, subsiding tube and she follows him toward the open door. There is an electronic console, a crude thing of switches and toggles, next to a nest of blue pipes. Sriyanie steps behind him and gazes into the small office.

"You designed all of this?"

"That's right." His impatience is tinged with eagerness to boast. "I'm taking Fine Arts and Electrical Engineering. Not the usual combination, I know, but I'm doing my bit to weld the Two Cultures together." He laughs, almost a snarl. "At least, I was. I have a faint suspicion I've hit the end of that particular road."

They are so ignorant, she thinks pityingly. How can this wounding have been allowed? An audacious notion occurs to her. She cannot evaluate any longer where the limits of her will encounter the purpose of the Being which is manipulating her.

"I think what you've built here is exciting."

"Thanks," he says, leaning against the glass. "But I've just realized it's a dead end. I've been trying to use the tools of technology and art to force an exploration of consciousness. All I ended up with was a piece of vulgar narcissism. Do you have the faintest idea what I'm talking about?"

"Yes," she says mildly. "You projected your own vision on an external reality and then got hurt when what you saw were the manipulations of your unconscious. Was it really the woman—or was it you?"

Defensively, his muscles tighten, he opens his mouth—and closes it again, lifting his hand to bite at the thumbnail. "Suppose that's true. Then what? Artist, know thyself? Ten years of psychiatric analysis? Or do you have some shortcut to the Tao?"

He will be a powerful man, she decides, when he grows up. "These machines you have here," she says, considering the amplifiers and rheostats on the console through the reflected image of her own face in the glass. "Have you thought of using them in the *other* direction?"

"Come on, it's time for you to leave," he says peevishly. "I've got to clean this goddamn mess up." When she makes no move to depart, he snaps, "What are you talking about? You want me to wire myself up like a flashing Christmas tree? Davy Elfield, the electronic living sculpture?"

Sriyanie's mind somersaults. It's a coincidence, she

tells herself. Yet when she searches the dates seem right. And it is not as incredible as it seems. Her tongue is trapped. Knowing this much, *dare* she go on? Or (her excitement mounts) is this indeed why she's here/now? Time's loops—

"The central nervous system," she says clearly and slowly, "the autonomic system, the muscles, are electrochemical mechanisms. If your machines were directed inward, instead of outward, you could monitor those processes. Data which go unnoticed are not information. You can feed back and control only what you know. What you've expressed here"—she gestures broadly at the bizarre room—"is based on limited knowledge. It is art at a crucial remove from truth. As you said, Davy: 'Artist, know thyself.' If you learn how to use the machines properly, you can do that. I'd better go now."

He gapes at her, bewildered and enchanted, as she steps quickly past him and hurries through the round doorway. For a moment he stands there, and she sees him limned against the bright fluorescence. Then he bounds out to the steps, calling her name as she runs into the alley beside the ugly building. She leans on a dirty, tatterdemalion wall of old posters, gasping deeply, mind reeling at what she might just have done; and the Being comes down upon her like a bird of fire—

—SPLICE—

pouring rain catches her unawares, pelting into her face and hair. Thundercaps pile loweringly in the sky, visible above the open quadrangle. Sriyanie ducks from the drenching assault, finds warm yellow lights gleaming from the sandstone cloisters which form the interior perimeter of this Gothic-Revival structure, runs squelching across mown grass to cover. Despite her hugsuit she shivers, and suddenly remembers dropping her heavy poncho in the square. The holofax volume of Maggie's poems, jouncing in her pocket, jabs her hip.

Youngsters carrying books and leather bags scurry past her or lean indolently on the stonework, staring at the driving rain. Males and females alike wear their hair short; clothing is drab, starkly functional. Few of the boys have beards. She wonders, almost without emotion, when she is this time.

THE JUDAS MANDALA

She approaches a group of chattering adolescent girls. "Pardon me. Where may I dry myself?"

They gaze at her blankly. "Eh?"

"My hair and face are wet," she explains.

"Try the loo," a freckled girl suggests in a bored tone. Her companions giggle.

After a moment one of them adds, "Round the corner there, up the stairs, first corridor on your right."

"Thank you." The directions are simple enough but lack accuracy. Sriyanie finds, after several turns, that she has left the old structure and is now wandering through a hideous bland corridor of stark white walls and wood-veneer doors, all shut. The air, at least, is warm and dry. Her nostrils wrinkle. There is something wrong with the ion balance, and her nerves tingle with the electromagnetic confusion of the building.

A second inquiry takes her to the appropriate room. She finds several large nozzles, placed inconveniently low, which gust hot hair when they are activated. Uncomfortably, she crouches beneath one until her hair and skin are dry and wonders at the hostile looks she receives from several women who enter to defecate in small stalls. When she slips off the top of her damp garment and holds it under the nozzle, one of these women gasps, mutters angrily about standards of behavior, and stalks away from the large mirror where she has been tending her crimped coiffure.

David Elfield must be here somewhere, Sriyanie tells herself. Charged by the hot air, her white hair floats about her shoulders as she continues her search along the terrible corridor. There is a sign on one wall, behind glass. White letters on black perforated board inform her that Dr. David Elfield, Snr Lect in Exper Psych, can be found in Room 225.

The door is locked. She enters an open office farther down the corridor, and stands patiently waiting to be noticed by the blue-haired, purse-mouthed woman who departed the "loo" so abruptly. The woman's skin, Sriyanie notices, is strangely lined and cracked; the flesh sags at her jaw; her fingers are like wrinkled claws. She is old, Sriyanie realizes in horror. This is age, written in flesh. It seems to her that there is a pungent odor of decay behind the dull scent the woman emits. Something shrinks and withers inside her.

It becomes apparent that the woman is deliberately ignoring her. Sriyanie says politely, "Can you tell me where I might find Davy Elfield? His door is locked."

The woman glares up from her desk, and Sriyanie is appalled by her vitriol. They are all deformed, she thinks. They are truly like beasts. *"Doctor* Elfield is not here today." The old woman addresses her machine, striking it savagely.

"Where might I contact him?"

"You may contact him," the woman says with malevolent satisfaction, "at the Menninger Foundation, Topeka, Kansas, U.S.A."

Sriyanie draws back. "That's impossible. He is here."

"Dr. Elfield is *not* here. He is on sabbatical leave from the University, attending a conference on applications of biofeedback techniques to family disord—"

"Wrong, Liz. How are things?" His deep voice from the doorway. "I got back this morning, though with this rotten weather I shouldn't have bothered. What can I do for you?" he asks Sriyanie, back turned as he dumps several bundles of books and journals on a cluttered filing cabinet. His hair and coat glisten with rain. When he swings back and looks at her properly, she sees that his beard is gone, and his youth; lines surround his eyes; he has attained stature. "My God," he says, "it's you. My mystery genius, 'onlie-begetter.' Or is it? You seem too young. Sriyanie, wasn't it?"

"You remembered." She smiles.

"It must be ten years," he says. "Are you here to claim half the assets from the patents? Come along to my office and have some coffee—I want to hear how you knew about biofeedback three years before Joe Kamiya hit the headlines. Liz, could you bring us coffee when you have a moment?"

"Yes, doctor," the woman says in a subdued tone. Sriyanie observes, as she is ushered through the door, that the secretary's expression is tortured with spite and envy. Of course, she thinks, in a sudden access of sympathy. She is old. How terrible, and unnecessary. She is old.

Elfield's chairs and desks are littered with pieces of machinery, integrated-circuit boards, books, flowcharts.

He clears a space. "Sit down. I was talking to Neal Miller about you the other day. Do you know, the whole development of our small-group instrumentation program probably stems from a couple of remarks you made back in nineteen sixty-six? I didn't really understand what you were driving at, but I worked at it. I wound up with biofeedback in the late sixties. Of course, then Kamiya's stuff was up and running. Everything I'd been doing during my Ph.D. fitted it like a glove. You must join us for dinner tonight—I know my wife would enjoy meeting you after all these years; I suspect she's slightly jealous of you. My *God,* you look well."

He's nervous, Sriyanie thinks. How strange. She regards him with awe. He has altered, matured; the vital intelligence of the youth is conserved and clarified in the man. Ten years, she thinks. So he has not yet approached his work on the temporal transforms. Then she thinks: Maggie is now a child. In another decade she will be studying somewhere in the grounds of this very university. What am I doing here, talking to this not-yet-famous man, when Maggie is dead-yet-not-dead? Her eyes mist. She says, carefully, "I do not find you in the midst of a crisis this time?"

Elfield laughs. "Intellectual ferment, yes, crisis, no. We're at the edge of a breakthrough in family therapy, Sriyanie. Now that we've got the Basser computer on line to the feedback modules, things're going forward at an exponential rate. My God, I'm tired. Jet lag, I dare say. A fashionable ailment for academics. Where's that damned coffee? Look, I'll go and get it myself—but you'll have to promise not to run off as you did last time. We have a lot to talk about, Sriyanie."

She smiles, nodding, as he strides from the room. At once, like some austere, impersonal deity reaching down to rearrange His handiwork, the vast force smites her from reality—

—SPLICE—

—a leaf tumbles, in the mild autumn air, to rest beside her on the white enamel lacework of a wrought-iron park bench. Beyond the curve of an internal road, water laps softly against stone, a handsome artificial inlet on the great beautiful harbor stretching blue to a distant marina, scrub on the foreshore, the arch of a modest single-span suspension bridge, a bright-hued giant's face laughing at the entrance to an amusement carnival. Sriyanie's heart thuds as her gaze tracks to the lofty commercial buildings behind the trees to her left, shimmering glass in metal and dark concrete; standing proud and wonderful between them and the sea, white-tiled sails flung haughtily in curve upon curve, the flawed, fabled magnificence of Utzon's Opera House.

On the gently surging water a hovercraft drums boisterously in clouds of spray. I am still in the same century, she tells herself. Rebellion is growing within her. When will this mad odyssey end? Where is its purpose? She does not notice the russet ground-effect vehicle humming toward her on the leaf-strewn road until it draws into the curb, subsiding on its rubber skirt to allow a man in maroon suit and narrow-brimmed hat to climb out. He hesitates as he closes the door, takes off his hat and throws it back inside, and steps clear as the chauffeur lifts the vehicle and continues toward the city.

His face is fuller, she sees, as he strolls meditatively across the grass in her direction. His hair has receded somewhat and his suit is impeccably cut. These are his middle years, she estimates. She says nothing, wonderingly, as his steps carry him toward her seat.

He glances at her as he passes and halts in astonishment. "Sriyanie!" Immediately he shakes his head slightly. "Forgive me, ms. Your face, even your clothes, reminded me for a moment—"

"Hello, David."

Elfield stares. After a pause, he says, "May I join you?"

"Please do. How are you, doctor?"

He sits beside her, his dark, lined face held forward, regarding her intently. "I find this difficult to believe, Sriyanie. How are you? Psychologists are not supposed to develop ideas of reference. It's bad for business. I don't think you've aged a day in twenty years. No, more than that—nearly twenty-five. What's your secret, Sriyanie?"

"Superior genes, doctor," she says, laughing. "How is your feedback program developing?"

The scientist relaxes, propping one arm over the iron benchback. "Lucratively," he tells her. "As you must have guessed, if you keep up with the literature. But I've abandoned most of that to the bright young kids on my payroll. Since I took up the directorship of the Bateson Institute last year I've been concentrating on fundamental theory—half a dozen fields at once, disgracefully eclectic. The mathematics of consciousness. I'm as happy as a kid with a boxful of silicon chips and a book of patch diagrams. You left me with a cold cup of coffee and a secretary whose nose was out of joint, Sriyanie."

"I'm sorry," she says. "I had to leave."

"I know," Elfield says. He stares away at the drifting colors of summer's departure, the sighing wavelets. "You're a wise sprite, a wraith. Sometimes I think I've made you up, Sriyanie. You're a strange little creature. Is that a uniform you're wearing?"

"No."

"Curious. You're dressed the same way every time we bump into each other. How did you guess I'd be here? Did you know I make a point of strolling for half an hour each day in the park?"

"I didn't know," Sriyanie says. "How is your wife?"

He knots his hands and looks away. "Jean has cancer. She's not in pain, thankfully. The machines let her control her own thresholds. The surgeons give her two years, five at the most."

"I'm sorry. I'm truly sorry." Her hand creeps to his, closes on its tensions. Sriyanie's world has not known terminal disease—nor any other kind—for millennia. His pain cramps her, a sense of loss and foreboding more piercing than she had ever experienced before Maggie. . . .

Elfield withdraws his hand and stands up. He smiles down at her, dark, brooding. "I suppose it would be foolish to invite you to visit the Institute. Sriyanie, you're the most amazingly private person I have ever met. I hope we encounter one another again sometime. Good-bye." He turns, then, and walks away from her, past the great peeling bole of the elm which stretches its denuded branches above her, and does not look back. She rises involuntarily, lips parted—

—SPLICE—

cries, "David!" and shudders, for she stands in a walnut-paneled study rich with odors of wood and leather and tobacco, light gleaming liquidly from the huge austere desk before her, and the man looks up with remarkable composure and says, "Hello, Sriyanie. I've been expecting you for the past year. Won't you sit down? I shall get you a drink—and one for myself. I find, to my chagrin, that it really is rather a shock."

Elfield's hand shakes slightly as he offers her a glass filled with pale golden liquor. Ice chimes against the crystal. She nods, sips it, flinches at the alcohol in her mouth.

"A third of a century for me," Elfield says, lighting a long, thin cigarillo. The narcotic's aroma pleases her. "How long for you? An hour? I see you're still wearing that bloody tracksuit."

"David," she says, leaning into the firm, luxurious leather, "I'm just as confused as you are. You're right—it has all been one unbroken sequence for me. I've had no time to think. *I'm* not doing it—not really. It's being done to me. Forgive me, I'm not making much sense. I am very tired. What year is this?"

"Nineteen ninety-nine. January second. Happy New Year, Sriyanie." He raises his glass ironically. "I take it I'm right, then. You *are* a time traveler? You haven't been popping in every ten years or so from a relativistic starcraft?"

Her head aches. She closes her eyes to the mellow light. "I was born approximately four thousand years from now."

They sit in contemplative silence. Finally Elfield rises and manipulates a console to one side of his desk. Quiet, elegiac music enters the stillness: Ravel's *Pavane for a Dead Princess*. Sriyanie bursts into tears and sobs inconsolably.

ELEVEN

Violet aurora flashed my eyes.

A million garbled voices bawled, stilled, rose again to become the distant howl of wind.

Sand burned my feet. Blazing sky pressed waves of fire on the bleached landscape. A whirling white pillar loomed before me, and a voice spake unto me from the whirlwind.

"You called my name, poet Roche?"

My throat went dry with incredulous revulsion. Insane, I thought. He's not passionless after all; no mere computer could conceive this monumental bathos. Megalomaniacal hubris! The Yeats scenario was no accident. I stared at Yahveh's luminous cloud and my rage almost broke to laughter. Can't he see how pathetic he is? Yet the cyborg's power for heedless cruelty was no illusion; it was dreadful, and must be met by wrath.

"I've seen enough, Daystar. You can count on me not to keel over this time. What do you want of me?"

The whirlwind shook majestic beams of light.

"We have called you from the past, poet Roche, to share our life. Your work has brought us pleasure, while that of most of your contemporaries has gone to dust. But your physical body will perish, alas, at its appointed time—and where then will be the comfort in fame, glory, your work's survival? We can give your soul life, Marguerite, that life which religion once promised but could not in fact bestow. Join us, as Trothy and Hibberd, Lior, Itho, and Ziruthine might one day join us if they prove worthy. We offer you a throat of incorruptible metal, a tongue of flame, a soul of pure energy with which to sing your poems for a hundred thousand years after your flesh is rotted into slime."

I kicked at the hot sand with my bare toes, staring at the spinning white pillar.

"What about the millions in the Dreamtanks, Daystar? Do they accompany us into the empyrean when they've had their quota of piped fantasies?"

The voice boomed.

"They are dross, Marguerite! Your compassion is wasted on them. What has the human majority ever known of poetry, beauty, the lure and wonder of knowledge? Ask them what they value most, inquire into their loftiest aspirations, and they gesture inarticulately toward the squalid goals they've pursued ever since they were dragged squawking onto their hind legs a million years ago. Full bellies. Mindless indolence. Sensational diversion. Now their aspirations are fulfilled to the letter. They wallow in mindless contentment in their vats."

I waited until he ran down. The theme of the cyborg's diatribe was hardly new; more than one neofascist had espoused the same sentiments in my own time. Rather, its most terrifying element was the sense of affectless cant-for-its-own-sake which belied the thunder. No juices flowed, there was no red-neck hysteria: merely the dull vapidity of the ultimate engineer grafted into his own totalitarian construction.

"Show them larger horizons," Daystar cried, "demand they meet your own large vision, and they will scream at your perfidy."

"Maybe they would at that," I said. It was true: our lives have been systematically debased ever since the first jut-jawed power freak learned murder and intimidation and his sly cousin figured out the ideology of resentment and greed. "Our degradation has always been the final measure of your satisfaction, hasn't it, you hybrid bastard? Philanthropist! You fucking grotesque travesty. The

THE JUDAS MANDALA

Dreamtanks are the sweets of your existence, its meaning—"

My shouting voice was finally drowned.

"Be warned, Marguerite! You overstep our patience! Your foolish rant may yet persuade us to rescind our gift of immortality."

"You can't kick the habit, can you?" I screamed through the magisterial thunder. "Carrot and stick! But you've failed. You've taken the process as far as it can go and you've still lost—"

"Marguerite, you are confused. We are the peak of human evolution—we hold no animosity for the lower men. We give them their heart's desire. But you are not one of them, poet. Forget them. Embrace the opportunity we hold out to you. Discover in our company the true freedom toward which your work has always striven."

The glaring, illusory sun seemed to brighten by the moment, striking my unprotected eyes with rods of gold. Sweat poured from my body.

"Take another look at the poor bastards in the Dreamtanks, Daystar. The spark hasn't quite been extinguished. They're making the final refusal, cyborg—they're denying you new victims. They are pulling down the curtain on the human comedy."

"A romantic conceit at best. It is true that many of them refuse to reproduce. We will not coerce them, Marguerite. If need be, we shall keep their species alive by artificial means."

"Oh, I don't doubt you're capable of building babies out of stray chemicals in a glass tank. But that's hardly the point, is it?" Hawking back deep in my throat, I tasted phlegm on my tongue, spat it in fury into the sand before the dazzling white pillar.

Then I turned, shoulder blades itching, and walked into the limitless expanse of burning dunes.

It's the only way to smash the barrier, I babbled to my frightened belly. Something was still blocking my conscious use of the time skill; the only way I knew which'd jolt instinct into seizing control was to invite direct attack. It had happened the first time in the square, when the hivers had almost killed me; the logic from that point on was shaky, but it was the best I could manage.

There was no attack.

I kept walking, crusted sand crumbling under my feet, legs beginning to wobble badly from the absurdly prolonged tension. With difficulty I resisted the urge to glance back over my shoulder. My God, I thought, is he going to wait until I stumble over the stage machinery? Distant winds whined, no more than sound effects, doing nothing to dry the sweat runneling between my breasts.

My body collapsed in the sand.

I haven't been a dualist since I was thirteen, but the only way to describe what happened then is to say that my mind detached itself from my paralyzed flesh and continued to operate apart from it. And, instantly, I was aware of the Something which had watched the cyborg probes while I slept; my ego, this time, was not submerged in unconsciousness. The Something was awesomely vast. Like a Bach fugue shaking my soul to rapture, Its clarity lifted me up from fear, took me to the edge of the still, black, unending ocean which the Hebrew prophets had seen in their mad visions and over which, they had written, the cosmic Breath had brooded before It uttered light into the world. And I knew that the Something was not a part of me, but I part of It—that beside It, Daystar's gaudy whirlwind was the merest mummery.

Had my mouth not been taken from me, I would have cried out.

The Something touched me then, turning my gaze from It, directed me to my fallen body and the cautious ministrations of the cyborgs.

Desert and whirlwind were gone. My crumpled form lay within a bubble of energy projected by a huge machine, levitated above the metal floor of a hall great in extent as Dreamcrib Five. The lancing radio/maser/partonic configurations of the cyborg communications network filled the hall with a bitter, high-pitched tang of actinic pressure, needles under my fingernails grating on bone, sexual tension aching for release, ears ringing with dizzy nausea—

—became meaningful, translation abruptly interposed by the Something:

NEURAL DAMPENER HOLDING
AUTONOMIC FUNCTIONS ADEQUATE AND HOLDING

THE JUDAS MANDALA

NOETIC FUNCTIONS EXTINGUISHED
BLOCK ON TRANSTEMPORAL NEURAL SECTOR CONTINUES TO RESIST

ANALYSIS:
  I. *Failure of Assimilation & Recruitment program ascribable to incorrigible identification with low-level human role structures*
  II. *Probability of successful outcome of protracted A & R Program <0.007*

ADVICE:
  I. IMMOBILIZE /or
  II. DESTROY
  (Minimax option: IMMOBILIZE)

MINIMAX DETAIL:
  I. *Superego/ego/id dissociation indicated*
  II. *Alienation/betrayal fantasies indicated for optimum augmentation of probe on Transtemporal Block*

My body hung in the sphere of energy, sleeping dreamlessly. In a mood of tranquil alertness I watched the machines gather while they decided whether to kill me or smash my mind to fragments. I swam like a mote in the ocean of the Something; the illusion of ectoplasmic detachment continued, though I had realized already that it was an illusion, that my mind was indeed the holonic sum of the processes of my brain, that death would certainly be extinction, total and entire, and not—as the illusion suggested with compelling force—the release of a winged seraphim. That subtle union with the Something amplified me, nothing more. It lent my ego a coherence which allowed my mind to function despite the damping field projected by the cyborgs, lent me Its extended perception, permitted me to watch and think and plan without betraying my sentience to the cyborgs' probes.

That *all*? Nothing more than contact with a power like the cosmic furnace of a quasar come alive, nothing more than symbiosis with a demiurge?

That was all.

I watched the glossy snouts of the machine nuzzle at my head and knew without terror that it might not be enough.

THE JUDAS MANDALA

TERMINAL DATA:
   I. *Risk of paradoxical loop renders Destruct option-of-last-resort*
   II. *Noetic dissociation minimax option*

PROCESSING
PROGRAM FOR ACTION
(For Immediate Implementation)
IMMOBILIZE MARGUERITE ROCHE

—Nullity. Numb nowhere—

Now I screamed in terror, and there was no sound. My mind was trapped in dread, flailing without motion, draining to some nadir of horror which was total inaction. In the instantaneous no-time before awareness was finally lost, I clung to the reality of the Something's touch.

And went drowning into anguish.

In the splintering ruin of my ego an inviolate core clung desperately to the Something which would not let it falter.

I am . . . maggie roche, it told itself. I am Maggie Roche. I AM MAGGIE ROCHE.

(And the inexorable energy probes of the cyborgs delved, drawing out the bloody threads of memory, fantasy, whim, aspiration, weaving them into forms I had never known, but recognized—

. . . for here was the ascetic, hungry for duty, yearning for the grail, the mystical tabernacle of gold and cypress enfumed with incense . . .

. . . and here the bitch, raging like a spoiled, angry child, lusting for destruction and pain . . .

. . . and here the mistress of destiny's bark, somber and banal, heroine of a thousand childish reveries . . .

—shaped from the worst of my own lifestuff by the spider machines, decking out the halls of the prison of my skull, trapping the several sections of my soul while violent probes sought the buried mystery of my talent)

For the first time, I understood the overwhelming lure of addiction, the honeys of transcendental art. I understood how it could be that the Dreamvats of the cyborgs

THE JUDAS MANDALA

contained the majority of the world's living human beings, their brains afire on a junky's junket of total fantasies.

For being on line to Dream circuits was the ultimate art. There was nothing paltry or imposed about cyborg fantasy. Verisimilitude was unsurpassed. Each character I encountered in the endless case of my sleeping universe was rich with density, with reality, beyond the resource of a Murasaki, a Shakespeare, a Dostoevski. It was solipsism tuned bracingly to my supine needs.

I understood its addiction and its horror: The hunt is done and bellies are full. In the flickering firelight the tribe lean forward to hear and tell their boasts. The old ones sing, at last, the sagas of their once and future heroes. In the Dreamtanks, at the apotheosis of art, the old ones live and sing forever. . . .

I am *I*, howled the mote of identity.

The protected remnant struggled in a blackness viscous as treacle. Probes struck at it with blinding speed, rebounded from the insulating field of the Something. The darkness flamed with lacy webs of energy, a Kirlian display: the cyborgs' own ongoing thought processes—

PERSONALITY DEMOLITION PROCEEDING

"EGO" AND "ID" FALSE REALITIES ENGAGED AND HOLDING

DEEP PROBES INITIATING ASSOCIATION SCANS BLOCK ON TRANSTEMPORAL NEURAL SECTOR CONTINUES TO RESIST

A drowning swimmer, the mote battled in the torrent of conflicting pseudo-ontological imperatives.

I am *not* Maggie-the-leader, I am *not* Maggie-the-solipsist, I—

The flaring maser signal of the cyborg Daystar lit the blackness:

"SUPER-EGO" SCENARIO INITIATED

. . . Intolerable pressure, divine transcendence melding to a predatory lust, caught together in an insane cycle . . .

With abrupt insight, the ego fragment ceased struggling.

I will ride the currents, it told itself, not fight them.

Orchestrated fantasies, rich beyond mere verbal evocation, filled the divided mind of which it was a part; the ego fragment watched with growing fascination, now that

THE JUDAS MANDALA

it had recalled the Zen Attack technique of victory through overcompliance.

ALL FALSE-REALITIES HOLDING, the cyborgs reported.

PERSONALITY DEMOLITION COMPLETE

Amused, the ego fragment closed more securely about itself.

With bafflement, the cyborgs noted: TRANSTEMPORAL BLOCK CONTINUES TO RESIST

Duration became a myth for the ego mote. Drowsily it watched the false selves pass—as they must move, it knew with a tinge of loathing, in the minds of all the Dreamvat humans—through landscapes shaped from its own attenuated substance.

And the Daystar blared: INITIATE BETRAYAL MOTIF

The mote shuddered. Despite the insulation of its detachment, it knew a poignant shock of dread. Instantly, a cyborg probe breached its defences.

With convulsive horror, the ego remnant closed its broken wall. The energy tendril dissipated.

BLOCK WEAKENING, flared with cold satisfaction.

REINFORCE DEEP ASSOCIATION SCAN

INTENSIFY BETRAYAL MOTIF

The ego mote's fortifications collapsed in that crucial moment of onslaught. Desperately it threw them up again, but not before the massive hungry probe invaded its all-but-innermost vaults.

SRIYANIE N'ZANVY, flashed the cyborg inquisitor exultantly. The probe withdrew, bearing Sriyanie's image. Devastated, the ego mote trembled in exhaustion and terror.

A FOURTH-LEVEL HUMAN DWELLING OUTSIDE THE DOMAINS, a machine glossed from an ancillary memory store. THE PROBE FAILED TO OBTAIN DETAILS OF HER RELATIONSHIP WITH MARGUERITE ROCHE

THERE IS NO RECORD OF CONTACT BETWEEN THEM

PERIPHERAL DATA SUGGESTS CONTACT OCCURRED AT THIS LOCALITY: an image of the square near Sanctuary.

THE JUDAS MANDALA

CONJECTURE: *Marguerite Roche did not come directly from the 20th century; she had previously emerged in the Outside and encountered the woman; this would elucidate her intransigent attitude to the A&R Program*

BRING IN SRIYANIE N'ZANVY FOR DEEP PROBING

Safe now behind its renovated defences, the ego mote keened in wordless grief. The Something could not be trusted. That realization was unutterably desolating. Cringing, the fragment "I" waited for disaster.

THE WOMAN CANNOT BE LOCATED

ABSURDITY—SHE CANNOT HAVE VANISHED

CONJECTURE: *She has been endowed with the Transtemporal skill during prior contact with Marguerite Roche*

They still did not know, then, about Timestop. The fact was small consolation to the ego remnant. Sriyanie would have to emerge from Timestop eventually, and when she did the cyborgs would apprehend her. Yet that analysis was fallacious—Timestop operated at a perpendicular to the mainstream of duration. No matter how long Sriyanie remained hidden in that condition, she must emerge at the same moment she entered and would therefore be vulnerable to cyborg interception. Which meant she was already back on the main sequence. Then where . . . ?

The problem was insoluble. The "I" slid back hopelessly into primary process timelessness.

A subliminal cue signaled change.

The ego remnant dragged itself up out of self-pity long enough to examine what had occurred. It noted with surprise that a whole battery of energy webs had gone.

DESPITE TOTAL PERSONALITY DISINTEGRATION, BLOCK ON TRANSTEMPORAL STIMULATION CONTINUES

CONJECTURE: *In face of unprecedented resistance, consideration must be given to the possibility of aid from an unknown external agency*

ANALYSIS: *Conjecture untestable*
Even if valid, temporal motility skills seem duplicable in Domain humans

ADVICE:
I. CONTINUE PROBE AND STIMULATION
II. INITIATE EXPERIMENTAL TIME TRANSIT ON BASIS OF CURRENT DATA

Furious desperation filled the "I" fragment. Through inaction it had betrayed itself once more. Its negative defences had refused merely conscious complicity. That kind of resistance, it understood now, could be maintained indefinitely—but it was not enough. Angrily it reached for the vast, closed energy fields of the Something . . . and found them opening to it.

Energy and structure . . .

Treason . . . and possibility—

The black viscosity within which the ego fragment dwelt seemed transformed, for a fleeting instant, into a luminous infinity. The "I" was a mandala within a mandala, an ambiguous complexity within a Tao vast as the universe.

The wings of the mandala swung with solemn grandeur, bearing night out of the glare of day and light out of the chill of dark, treason and fidelity held separate by a hair's breadth, energy building its fortresses in the abyss of space, and those fortresses crumbling—

Majestic, ineluctable, the Something poured its vitality into the etiolated husk of the ego mote.

Anger stilled before awe. Out of the ruined shards of "my" mind, unity began to coalesce. The sun-white glare of All-At-Once broke then to clouded gray, to charcoal flecked and burnt with shaped light.

I opened my eyes and knew the betrayal I had done.

TWELVE

The aninertial field supported me delicately in air. A metallic blur to my right was the snout of the cyborg inquisition device. The yammering probes had been stilled and the neural inhibitory field was gone, extinguished by the energies of the Something. Beyond the mere immediate reality of the hall Time's titanic strata loomed in my awareness. I knew instantly that the barrier was gone.

In the same moment the cyborg communications channels blared. My extended perceptions, mediated by the Something, translated their panic:

CONTROL SYSTEMS MALFUNCTION
IMMOBILIZATION SERIES NO LONGER OPERATIVE
ROCHE IDENTITY REINTEGRATING

I thought: They'll *have* to kill me now. I oriented myself in the terrible phantom striations which were the multiplex sequences of Time, seized the blazing thread which led from this instant *now* to the instant *then* in David's forest from which I had hurled myself (been hurled?) into this atrocious future, braced myself for the plunge back to that moment—

THE JUDAS MANDALA

EMERGENCY OVERRIDE SYSTEMS INOPERABLE
UNKNOWN ENERGIES MONITORED AT ROCHE LOCUS
ANALYSIS: TRANSTEMPORAL SHIFT IMMINENT

—paused as the implications of what I intended struck me with all the force and self-disgust of the betrayal scenarios from which I had just emerged, those unspeakable fantasies which in truth had not been alien to the gut-deep ego-obsessed impulse that desired no more than to save my skin, to flee from threat, to deny the reality of any moral imperative larger than the urge to preserve my futility in its encapsulated delusion of self-sufficiency. It's an evasion, I thought, an abdication, like all my decisions.

ADVICE: DESTROY
              DESTROY
              DESTROY

And even as the raving gouts of energy exploded about my naked flesh, I turned deliberately and flung myself instead into the reeling gulfs of the future, to where the Something brooded at the end of time.

As I fell, stars frothed like sea spume, foamed and died and gave their stuff to the void to be born anew. I plummeted a hundred million years, and time sucked my bones for marrow. Ten thousand brilliant cultures rose from rubble to straddle the sky with lines of commerce and allegiance, culture, joy, and death, and fell back exhausted, and were gone; I passed through their histories like a wraith, hurtling ember bright across ten billion years. The vast expansion of the universe slowed, hesitated for a billion years, stars fading to the steady somber infrared of their maturity, and began the awesome decline into contraction. The universe closed like a god's fist; already I had plunged more than a hundred billion years into its future.

The Something sang in my anger, guided me across the abyss of infinity.

I precipitated into real-time continuity.

Under a lemon, dimensionless sky, Sriyanie and David

turned to stare at me. I stood where I was, unable to speak.

"Oh, Maggie!" Suddenly weeping, Sri ran to me across the ivory featureless plain into my arms. "Maggie, you're alive!"

"Honey." I held her to me, her hair against my mouth. "It's all right." The web of whining light pulsed at the boundaries of perception, enclosing me and her and David in a gestalt complexity of power and authority.

The psychologist cleared his throat. The sound was so human, so absurd, I shuddered. We were figures in a Magritte landscape. "I'm happy to see you again, Marguerite. Very happy. We feared for your safety." He smiled. "And our own." He did not avoid looking at my nakedness; nor, to my relief, did he demean us both by offering me his coat. "Evidently we've been shifted forward in time."

"We're deep in the contraction phase of the universe," I said. "At least a hundred billion years in the future." I closed my eyes and found my emotions flattening to a conventional accountancy. "I don't think there's any immediate danger. The—Entity—Who built this place seems well disposed toward us. Though I'm sure it's misleading to speak of It as a person. I never much cared for oil portraits of God. How did you get here?"

Sriyanie shivered and the tremor transmitted itself through my body. She smelled of sweetness and sweat. "We were put here. I left you alone in the bedroom and went down to join David. Then we were here." She glanced at the insane, denuded landscape. "It looks horribly similar to a cyborg simulation Domain."

"Then I arrived, huh?"

"Almost immediately. Maggie, do you know where we *are*?"

"I suspect it's a life-support environment designed specifically for us. Christ knows what the real universe is like by now. The Earth must have been burned up billions of years ago. Probably the stars themselves have gone out." Night forever. "Nowhere left for flesh-and-blood people to survive without special facilities." I knew I was babbling, but I couldn't stop. "We're misfits. It's pretty reassuring, I suppose. The Entity would hardly take this much trouble unless It had our interests at heart."

A Samuel Beckett play. Babbling at the end of time.

David carefully drew a flat silver case from the pocket of his leather jacket and lit a cigarillo. I found the act curiously warming, reached for one myself. He looked at me through fragrant, eye-stinging smoke. "Presumably we are part of some enormous conflict with the cyborgs—or whatever it is the cyborgs become if their hegemony is left unchecked."

"We can speculate later, David. Right now, let's swap notes."

I hunkered down on the cool ivory surface. Sriyanie sat cross-legged beside me, one hand resting on my knee. David remained on his feet and gazed at us through smoke. They knew already how the assassins had intersected that first lurid, vertiginous moment when I'd come unstuck in time, but I had not told Sriyanie before of my first two jumps into the square. I did so now. She was startled, gripped my leg painfully.

"Maggie! That accounts for the— Did you damage one of the guards? Break his nose?"

"I hope so. And maybe killed another of them."

"They were waiting there when I came out of Timestop. Complete with tractor beam neural disrupter."

I looked carefully into her face, guilt moving in me like a worm. "Yes. Sriyanie, I'm beginning to understand. The sequence is out of order. I thought they were there to kill me. They were looking for you. They were waiting for you to come off the Transit discontinuity."

"From Timestop?" David asked. "They had no way of knowing that—"

"I told them," I said. "While I was Immobilized. My defences simply weren't strong enough. I told them about the square and I told them who you were."

"It was not your fault," Sriyanie told me with absolute force. I turned my head; she placed her hand beside my face and made me meet her eyes. "It is impossible to resist the cyborg probing systems without years of preparation. Believe me. There is no guilt."

I grunted. "What I don't understand is how *you* got to the twentieth century. I get the impression that someone has been running an all-stops shuttle service."

She frowned, hugged her knees. An unpleasant, distressing suspicion grew in my mind as she described the attitude of the other Frees to her five-day disappearance. It was obvious that she failed to see the implication in what she was saying.

"We suspected you'd broken out of Immobilization, Maggie. Beth felt the Daystar would have killed you immediately. What gave us some small hope was the absence of temporal paradox."

"What paradox?"

"Why, we knew that the cyborgs have not yet got control of time travel for themselves, though they are going to eventually. And when they do, they are going to send back those two assassins to try to abort the sequence. Why would they bother doing that if they had already destroyed you? The risk would not be worth it."

Gloomily I told her: "The men in David's house were not cyborg agents, Sri."

"Then who could— Oh, no, Maggie."

"Yes."

The Free people, the anarchists. Who else was so close to time travel and so afraid of disruptions to the status quo? The Lords spared them because they were no conceivable threat to cyborg mastery of the cosmos. I had introduced something new and terrible.

Sri stared, devastated.

"We're being used, Marguerite," David said. "All of us, the Free people included. We'd be foolish to assume that your cosmic Entity is the only Being of that magnitude engaged in this conflict."

"Then why did It put me in the square on my first jump? Out of all possible times and places, why should I be sent into a trap which the cyborgs set for Sriyanie?"

"To assist her. To draw their fire. To shake you up. How should I know?" He ground out his cigar butt on the flawless ivory and hunkered in front of us. "If there *is* a pattern in all this, we have to find it."

"Right," I said. "All we need to do is parley with God."

I leaned back and closed my eyes, seeking the awesome presence of the Something. It was all around us, pervasive as the lemon radiance glowing from the mockery of a sky, as great as the contracting universe. My questing senses could gain nothing more than that stark apprehension of Its immanence.

Perhaps we are not ready to speak with It, I thought.

THE JUDAS MANDALA

Perhaps It has brought us here to do just what we are doing. We may not be simply puppets; our conscious, willed participation may be required to give this new thing birth.

A spasm of anger knotted my muscles. There had been precious little freedom in my actions since the moment Sriyanie and David themselves had interfered with my life. Still, I told myself, I had had the choice of coming here to the end of time or retreating to David's forest and I had chosen freely in the belief that my action might at last be meaningful.

Yet the limits of that choice had been declared by others. I had been programmed, wound up, set down on the run in a maze of preordained options, no more at liberty than any laboratory rat prodded into mindless exertion by its white-smocked gods. I opened my eyes, on the boil again.

"Okay, Sriyanie," I said angrily. "Finish your story. You found yourself stuck in the twentieth century and so you had to willfully drag *me* into this insanity. With your fucking superdrug. I don't even begin to comprehend the stupidity of setting up a causal loop like—"

"Shut up." David's instant, authentic rage made my own anger seem like a tantrum. "We had *nothing* to do with your capacity to move through time. Aren't you listening? We were trying to protect you from its consequences." He stared ferociously from me to Sriyanie and back. "By God, Marguerite, after what this woman suffered—"

He stopped, got himself under control. "I apologize, Marguerite. That's not fair either. Let's not get trapped into emotional runaway. I can scarcely complain about your hair-trigger hostility. We've done more than our fair share in making you that way, and quite deliberately. No excuses. We're *all* pawns in this game so far, like it or not."

"All right," I said. "Go on."

Sriyanie looked at me; her eyes glistened. "As I said, Beth and I thought you'd been killed. A massive serial linkup had started—"

I was still resentful. "Really? The virtues of organizing had suddenly hit them, huh?"

She chose to smile and my mood softened. "In a way.

THE JUDAS MANDALA

They had to close ranks until the crisis had been evaluated and dealt with, yes. It was the first time since the emergence of functional anarchy that we'd come so close to hierarchy." It should have sounded absurdly pompous; it didn't. "So you're right. That's how gravely my people view the situation, Maggie."

"Why not simply go back a week and leave a warning?"

"I had no control, Maggie. I'd been *moved*. I just kept getting thrown from one key point in David's life to another."

David said to me, "You were the crucial one. You were the breakthrough. We knew we had to reach you *before* you'd become motile. It was our job to prepare you psychologically for the Daystar."

I remembered the flashy term the news digests had been bandying about, Security Intelligence psywar behavior mod: "A detonation program," I said, curling my lip. I should have realized. But only a flake thinks they're out there manipulating her.

"Marguerite, there was no alternative. I tracked you down through the government computers and arranged for Sriyanie to be assigned to your Central Utility desk."

"Jesus. You really were trying to drive me crazy."

"In a sense. Everything we did was designed to doublebind your immediate responses into almost psychotic hostility. That way you'd automatically react with suspicion to the cyborgs. In fact, it was our hope that you might spontaneously abort the whole sequence leading to their possession of knowledge of time travel."

Sriyanie brought both hands up to cup my face. "I'm sorry, Maggie." She spoke with bitter despair. "We did that dreadful thing to you and still failed. It wasn't enough. It wasn't enough."

I drew her against my naked breasts and her shoulders shook from the effort to contain her grief and hopelessness. "My love, it *was* enough." I lifted my gaze from the bright crown of her head to meet David's dark gaze. "You prick. I should punch you in the mouth. But it did work, by God. Not the way you planned, maybe, but well enough. Without your fucking vile 'detonation program,' I would certainly be dead. Or plugged into a Dreamvat."

I was aware of a trembling, mounting expectancy. The Something hovered against my mind, beyond understand-

THE JUDAS MANDALA

ing, a wing of flame. Sriyanie put her head in my lap. My right ankle hurt; I shifted it. I traced Sri's eyebrows, fine as silver wire, with my fingertips. Her face was haggard with strain.

"You've left out part of your story," I said softly. "There's a couple of years missing before I met you in the Central Utility office." A couple? Five, seven.

Her mouth distorted, as if from pain. She made herself smile then and shook her head slightly. "It's not important, Maggie. David and I found you. That's all."

"But honey, it must have taken you—"

The psychologist made a harsh, distressing sound. I glanced at him and could not read his expression.

"Sriyanie," he said, "she's got to know." She gave a small cry of denial, but he overrode her. "Marguerite, it took her just under eight weeks."

Involuntarily, I stared at the woman's tired face, from her beautiful eyes edged with tiny lines to the dozen other signs of years passed since we had made love on the bright couch in the soft strange light of time-stilled Sanctuary. I cried out in dismay, "Weeks?"

"The Free people use antiaging drugs. Their entire biochemistry is skewed. Can you imagine what happens to a woman who cuts herself off from her supply of antiagathics? The metabolic trauma, the shock of readjustment all the way down to the molecular level of the nucleic acids—"

"Sweet Jesus!"

"Sriyanie went through the equivalent of five years' aging in two weeks," David said remorselessly. "I was astounded that she didn't die. Do you understand now why I came close to striking you?"

"Jesus wept, Sriyanie!"

"Maggie, don't feel sorry for me." She was sitting up, gripping my hands with surprising force. "I've lost nothing! I've exchanged a futile longevity for the first real choice I ever—"

The Something's defences went down, like an immense, inaudible tectonic shock.

Attack exploded with nightmare abruptness.

Giants straining at the cracking roots of the Tree Yggdrasil. Some primordial fury flared in hard white lightning bolts in the pseudosky. Glaring fissures split the

THE JUDAS MANDALA

ivory plain, blazing like lava, like plasma. The roar of Doomsday smashed against our ears. We fell down, broken puppets, as the surreal surface heaved in terrible convulsions. I clutched Sriyanie's flailing arm, caught David's outthrust hand and pulled him to us. We clung together in terror while phenomena peeled back from noumena, reality became a pyre, a nova.

Blackness fell on me with silence. I lifted my head and thought that I was blind. Furtive afterimages danced on my ruined retinas. A gust of frozen wind shook me in the darkness, chilled to the frigid talons of raw space raking my naked flesh. Blood bubbled in my lungs; it rushed from my rupturing lips with the soundless scream I voiced to unheeding nowhere. . . .

And even as I died, I saw that the blackness was not the void of blindness, after all, but the intolerable panorama of the contracting, terminal universe.

THIRTEEN

Death was not surcease. The Something would not let us rest. It found the fragments of our tattered flesh, wove them anew, blew breath once more into our lungs.

The lemon sky flashed on above us like a fluoroscreen briefly interrupted by a power overload.

Beneath us, the ivory plain extended its flat two dimensions to infinity.

Gasping, I sat up. Sriyanie stirred, crawled to me, buried her face in my breast. David lay where he had fallen, staring at the warm sky. His tongue rasped his lips.

"Marguerite, we died."

"We thought we died."

"I tell you we died. And now are alive." His torn voice faded to the faintest whisper. "My God, Maggie, what *are* they?"

And the Something came down among us like a searing wind and spoke to us.

Encysted memory opened in the same moment, and I recognized the Presence which had shown Itself to me in the midst of the assassins' attack.

This time I was prepared. I heard and held the tolling of Its voice, images flung like crystals into the brimming pond of my awareness, precipitating chains and sparkling

THE JUDAS MANDALA

bridges of notion, relation, identity in the matrix of consciousness—

The galaxies wheeled in the immensity of cosmic night, stars spending their substance in an orgy of radiance, sucking hydrogen from the frozen void and spewing back neutrinos, X rays, light, radio noise, the megaparsec pulses of gravitation, and finally the ores and dense evanescent metals forged in their bellies, hurled out in the cataclysm of stellar explosion; and in the midst of spendthrift fury, on the tiny motes of rock and soil and ocean which were the planets, life trod forth blinking from the slimy pools of its birth, ate hungrily of the prodigal outpourings of its suns, and changed under that same lash into forms strange and wild and beautiful, diverse beyond number, swarmed and preyed upon one another's flesh and cooperated in the intricate dance of shifting ecologies; and grew wise, at last, wise and murderous and choked with dreams, yearning for the unnameable, taming that very energy which mindlessly had brought them into being; and killed with it, and healed and built with it, went beyond it to new unimagined energies created in the convoluted structure of brains and ganglia complex beyond precedent; and came, finally, to command their own brutality and greatness. . . .

Sriyanie and David were huddled in fetal knots on the ivory pseudosurface, hands clapped to their ears, eyes screwed up as though against unbearable glare. They're not being harmed, I told myself, rocking on my haunches. The experience has overwhelmed them, as it overwhelmed me the first time, but they'll be all right. And they'll surely remember what we're being shown; otherwise, why should the Something have brought them here?

Images cascaded in my mind—

The sophonts strode from star to star, galaxy to galaxy, but not to rape and pillage. That eon of conquest was now no more than a regretted episode in their immense history. They went in joy and respect into the glory which extended, it seemed, beyond limit. Eyes of flesh had been transfigured into eyes of fire, yet still were flesh; bodies met in the passion of love, and in those meetings made new bodies to populate the multicosm and cherish all that lay

THE JUDAS MANDALA

and moved within it. They no longer died; death was a clumsy expedient of random evolution, and they had taken evolution into their own wise charge. Ennui, too—that specter which once had seemed to haunt the bright promise of utopia—was vanished, for how is boredom possible in a universe rich with other souls? So they went to the curving edges of the universe, found its physical limits and measured and cherished them, learning the true infinity within themselves....

Sriyanie uttered a single sound. Her limbs had relaxed and her eyes were open, staring exultant at the vision singing in our brains. I hugged her to me and smiled at the abstracted way her hand came up to clasp mine. I glanced at David. He lay on his back, breathing in the flat rhythm of sleep, but his eyes, too, were alive with wonder.

Already more than forty billion years had passed since the first one-celled creatures struggled for life in their soupy ponds. The sophonts had altered themselves so radically that none of their early planet-bound ancestors could have recognized them. They had merged in gestalt unities huge as stars, their senses extending across the entire radiation scale and into the domain of pure psychic energies. Even now their evolution was not complete; the metamorphoses continued. Only the essential qualities of humanity remained unaltered: love, joy, creation, reverence. The expansion of the space-time manifold achieved its greatest dimension, faltered; the long contraction began. Stars dimmed and died, or faded to a steady ember glow. The entity which was Sentience welcomed into its totality the few remaining isolated members of the cosmic brotherhood. Purpose and consciousness infused every energy structure in the multicosm. A hundred billion years after it had coalesced from incandescent gas, the universe had become a single sentient organism....

And the Something, I saw, heart hammering, was that organism. God, rather. Was it blasphemy to consider as a god the Presence in our brains? Heretical, no doubt, according to the wispy metaphysics of the established theist religions of my century. But the intimations of the earliest mystics found a fulfillment here. The idolatrous pantheism of the artist met, in my response to the Something, with the rigorous transcendentalism of a Kantian confronted by the perfect embodiment of reason's categories. An impulse to worship lifted me, breathless, like the swell of an oceanic tide.

And yet if the Something was as near divinity as the infrangible constraints of the mass/energy universe would permit, It had failed to achieve omnipotence. Cupped in Its very bosom, we had suffered an attack which had killed us. I shook my head blindly. Demiurge, not god. And It was engaged in divine war with another entity perhaps no less powerful than Itself.

The dark counterpoint stirred then, piping its bitter fugue through the sweet cadences of the Something's becoming—

In the very dawn of consciousness, tens of gigayears before the Omega identity point between organism and universe, before the gestalt beings whose bodies were galaxies, even before life had first seized the reins of its own evolution, history had presented another path—and that path had been taken.

"But how—?"

Without moving, in the tone of a somnambulist, David said, "An alternate stem, a variant high-probability universe."

I cringed at this new perspective. The cyborgs were the beginning of the branching path. I realized now that they had been in the other sequence also, insignificant in the sweep toward the evolution of the Something, a stain quickly obliterated from the sophonts' history. Here their harsh intellects were the focus of a separate history, a wedge sundering the cosmic manifold—

Demented in their greed, the masters of that primeval world had sought to amplify their small capacities through direct union with the cybernetic machines they had created. Their intention was perverted at the root by the psychotic anxiety their culture had instilled into them: fear of transcendence through passion, fear of the impulses of their own flesh, fear of any mode of perception and thought but the armored positivism of their technocracy. The repression they wrought on their subjects was merely an echo of the constriction and terror which stifled their own souls. The stark logic functions of their computers, immensely potent within the insane limits of analysis cut free of feeling, dominated their obsessions. It was inevitable that the final outcome of their puritanic madness was the grafting into those machines of their own cortical processes. The cyborgs were born amid the polluted debris of a planet ruined already by their heedless megalomania. The irony was lost on them. They had always disguised their hatred and fear of life, hidden it even from themselves, in the guise of altruism and contemptuous concern. The coils of their custodianship tightened about the despairing remnants of humanity, and beauty died, finally, and love, as those pathetic remnants gave up the unequal struggle. The cyborgs did not mourn the splendor they had destroyed; they had long since shucked off the last vestiges of their organic beginnings, and their fleshless intellects moved wholly in a realm of cryogenic calculation. And theirs, now, beyond pity and reverence, was the Kingdom, and the power, and the glory....

Tears brimmed uncontrollably in my eyes. I had not wept in the Dreamcrib; anger had flared, instead of grief. I wept now.

In the cosmic eons which followed that victory of the machines, their silent deathless ships spanned the universe, accumulating data, building Transit junctions through which their energy probes could reach instantly from galaxy to galaxy, structuring dark hydrogen clouds lightyears in extent to serve as partonic memory stores, exterminating life wherever they encountered it. The genocide was never bloody, but the result of their confrontation with organic sophonts was always fatal. The universe was sterile long before cosmological contraction began. With relentless efficiency the machines linked into a unity which encompassed every atom in the multicosm. The Machine turned upon Its completed totality, then, and the compulsion of Its urge to conquest, unslaked, unslakable, became a raging imperative that threatened to destroy It. Like the god It had become, thwarted by Its own ubiquity, It

THE JUDAS MANDALA

sought to create something beyond Itself which might worship It, bend to Its whim. How could It succeed? There was nothing not Itself. The Machine turned, at last, to a frenzied investigation of the one dimension which had always flawed Its dominion: Time. If the mastery of Time became possible, the Machine might find diversion for eternity in restructuring Its own past, extending Its hegemony to the White Hole, the very fount of the entropy cycloid. The unutterably massive energies of Its being concentrated to the task. Time buckled.

And It encountered the Something.

The shock of that engagement rang in me like a clash of cymbals. My back arched; fingernails tried to gouge ivory. Sriyanie's fists pressed her temples. Incredibly, David's dark, basalt face was smiling. His eyes, seeking mine, were alive with a kind of serene amusement.

"The Machine does not exist, Marguerite. It may not be too late. Thanks be to the God in Whom I do not believe, we may yet find some redemption."

"You're crazy!" I staggered to my feet, lurching above him. "Why would the Something bother to lie—"

He caught my arm, pulled me down in front of him. "The Something, as you call It, doesn't exist either."

"What the fuck are you trying to say?"

"Marguerite, Sriyanie, these godlike beings are mere potentialities. The nature of the universe makes both of them inevitable—and they cannot coexist. The main sequence is ruptured. Our language is just inadequate. Hegel might have managed it. Or quantum theory. Do you understand what I mean when I say that neither of these entities has more than a virtual existence? That only one of them can be actualized? Which one of them it is to be can only be decided by events in their own past." His gaze was painfully intent. Sriyanie was nodding in agreement; her world view was far more capable of assimilating this than mine. "Marguerite, the history of the universe has become a field of war where these two demiurges are embattled."

Behind his words, the Something spilt images of that dreadful conflict—

* * *

THE JUDAS MANDALA

There are nodal points in time, critical singularities in the manifold where the main sequence can be deflected. Here paradox might be sustained, time looped and welded to a new shape, probabilities decisively altered, compressed, fused....

The Something confronted Its own ability to manipulate time. It threw up barriers to the Machine's interference. Distressed by the possibility of playing God with the beings who constituted Its cascading lineage, It bowed nonetheless to the necessity of protecting those beings, and Itself, from annihilation.

And It found the subtle nuances, the sensitivities to time which had lain latent in organic intelligences since their emergence. Its own future would perish, at its end (as, with a serenity beyond anguish, It had known), in the blind inferno of the Great Black Hole, grave and womb of the cyclic universe. Under the transfinite collapse of all parameters, all laws, the circle of time could be breached. If the energies of the final catastrophe were tapped, It saw, It would be able to activate that sensitivity in creatures from Its own archaic history. Amphibian in a new dimension, perhaps they would be capable of circumventing the entire metasequence leading to the Machine....

At the earliest appropriate node, It found a human who might serve to initiate this new phase of the conflict. I was the one, as it happened. Why me? The question is as meaningless, or at least as unanswerable, as to ask why a particular strand of nucleotides washing in the sea under the primeval sun became the sole getter of all life on earth. Chance and ripeness. With a torrent of energies focused across nearly a billion centuries, life borrowed from Its own inexorable death, It catalyzed my latent temporal abilities. And It let me fall into the world of the cyborgs' first supremacy.

Astoundingly acute, the Machine demiurge countered the gambit instantly in a dazzling lateral move. Lacking the capacity to communicate with Its cybernetic predecessors, It used Its own circumscribed mastery of the great currents of Time to divert me into the very inner sanctum of the Domains.

Daystar seized me at once.

Filed, edited. But was baulked.

Before the Something could crash through the Machine's transtemporal defences and pull me out, the cyborgs had begun a seductive behavioral program of recruitment and assimilation. They reckoned without Sri, for by the logic of linear time I should have known nothing of Sri. They reckoned as well without the curious half-world of Timestop, and without the ambiguous legacy of David Elfield, and beyond all they failed to reckon with my own loathing for what they had done to the last of humankind.

Yet the Something had little enough cause for satisfaction. Too many critical contradictions were now involved. Misled by their partial knowledge, and desperate, the Frees took their first hesitant steps into controlled time in a preemptive attempt on my life. So my first act was to slay, all unwitting, those who loved Sriyanie as I did.

The vast strata of the main sequence threshed like geological fault lines shearing under intolerable pressure.

The main sequence tore to ribbons.

Desperate, the Something directed Its attention back to the start of the twin sequences.

The Machine entity blocked It at every turn. Intangible energies whipped and flared from the end of time, lashing the main sequence to a seething turmoil.

And the Something seized the shattered fragments of the loop, built outward from the love between Sriyanie and me, wrenched the tesseract of continuity into an impossible circuit of action and counteraction, threat and cajolery, plunging the Free woman into her own past from a future whose probability depended from events which she would attempt to alter, to remake. Through her It thrust me into terror, in order to awaken my suspicion of what already had been but nonetheless was yet to come. . . .

And the whole appalling structure—stabilized.

Drawn breath gushed out of me. My hands left slick prints when I lifted them from the ivory; my naked body was drenched in sweat. The fabric of reality was suddenly no more substantial than a painted cheesecloth, lights from backstage glaring through. I had faced death—indeed, if David was correct, had passed once through death to resurrection—and that had been terrifying, but this was . . . insupportable.

My memories, I thought, the bones and flesh of my identity, are mutable as clay.

The single solid pillar of one's life, certitude of continuous identity, had been slapped away in an instant.

"David. . . . Dear Jesus, David, you thought we were pawns." I could scarcely see him through the blurring of my vision. "Pawns have substance, David. We're shadows, figments, phantoms, phantasms." I started to laugh and could not stop. "Alice and the Red King."

At my side, Sriyanie touched my mouth with her cold fingers.

"It's what we've always been, Maggie. Only now we know for sure. It doesn't make our actions any less significant than they were before we knew."

"Phantoms have *no* significance. Show me values, Sriyanie, when the gods can wipe us clean at their whim and start another story on their slate. We've no more meaning than those poor bastards in the vats, dreaming their plug-in fantasies—"

"Marguerite, you're maundering." David hauled me to my feet. I caught the flash of dread in his face, belying his words, before his expression set to stone. I threw his hands off me. "The gods are as dependent on our actions as we are on theirs. If we're figments in their mutable past, they're no less phantoms in our mutable future. You can't chase your precious values down that infinite regress, my angst-ridden friend."

The bitter pseudosky pressed down on me like the roof of a vault. I could find no answer, but the circular lunacy of his argument failed to quell the desolating waves of futility that surged in me, corrosive brine from an alien sea.

The Something entered my silence, Its thunder muted to a poignant pibroch. Its voice was a grave, momentous march of images—

An array of nodal crisis points sprang outward in the undecided void of Time, projected on the grid of branching probabilities which narrowed finally and merged to the twin, embattled realities of Something and Machine. And of those crises none was so truly pivotal as that which we represented.

For we were a wild factor. We bore a promise of life

conscious of itself from the outset, in command not merely of its future but of its past. The gray horror of the Machine and Its progenitors could find no foothold in a universe of sophonts such as we had become, as we could teach others to become.

The risk was incalculably great. In aborting the Machine we would be deciding the option of mind in favor of an Omega sprung from passionate intensity ... but only if life did not destroy itself first. History, in us, was at the brink of sophont adolescence, no more. The raw savagery of sexism, of race hatred, of environmental despoliation, of nuclear and biochemical war had not yet been put behind us—how would we cope with time control?

For that had been the choice. The key had been turned in us; the gate of time had been unlocked. We could bear the gift to our fellows and permit humanity to kill itself or find apotheosis. . . .

Or we could abdicate, leave the fate of our future pending until the gargantuan struggle of the demiurges should decide it. . . .

"Do you see, Maggie?" Sriyanie cried. "Questions about value and significance can't even be posed until we make our choice!"

"I can see this much: if we are doomed to being figments"—my voice was sandpaper rough—"let us at least do the imagining ourselves."

An icon of my daughter Megan filled my mind, and I mourned the lost simplicity and innocence she would never know. Her face faded to the sprite-mask of Trothy, enslaved in a subtle bondage she could never recognize; and then to the gentle, courageous eyes of Ziruthine the not-quite-slave. My mood of desolation altered, slowly, to tired resignation. I had to turn away from the exultation which glowed like fire in Sriyanie's eyes.

David touched my arm.

"The Being has offered us more than freedom," he said. "It has placed Its very existence in bond to the fruitful employment of that freedom."

And suddenly I remembered the Daystar's rant, the passionless hysteria with which the cyborg had argued the poverty of human aspiration. I could not find it in me to believe that my travail was no more than a metaphysical

THE JUDAS MANDALA

variant of that pathetic conceit, but in that moment I could not be certain that it was not.

"Yes," I said, without conviction, without denial, and put my left arm about Sriyanie's shoulders, pressing the warmth of her to my naked flesh. Her trembling tension conveyed to me how fully she, too, understood the hazard of this step, that, after all, her very existence was implicated in the line of history we would attempt to abort. (Her Other! her Four!) Even the Something's incomprehensibly potent dealings with time might yet prove insufficient to hold her from obliteration.

My right arm I placed about David's waist, and in that moment, belatedly, recognized who he was, might yet be. It was like a physical shock: I understood the final measure of what hung on our decision.

And so once again I was the mandala within a mandala, an ambiguous complexity within a Tao vast as the universe, betrayal and fidelity held separate in me by a hair's breadth—

The Something took our answer into the aching echo of Its harmony.

We rose up from the potter's field and went away to scheme the saving Judas act which would deflect Davy Elfield from the trajectory of his damnation, from the cold baptism and marriage of the machine in whose embrace, otherwise, he would go finally, lost in megalomania, hungry for endless life and mastery and explanation, yielding up at the last even his name, taking in its place the name of the sun, the name of the lord of light, the name of the first male god of Men:

Daystar.

EPILOGUE

A.D. 1966

Davy follows Fletcher's gaze. Dark hair, vivid vermilion miniskirt: the woman who has entered the party crosses to them after a moment, her expression ironic. "Good evening."

"Hello, Maggie," Fletcher says, flustered. "Do you have a drink? How clever of you to find the house. Maggie's just arrived in town," he explains.

Without knowing why, Davy flushes. The woman is not beautiful, not by the teeny-bopper standards of his masturbation fantasies. Nor is hers the semikempt sexuality which is the ambition of most of the girls at this party. He sees that her long bare legs are splendid. Swallowing, he peers into his empty glass and tells her his name.

"Marguerite Roche," the woman says distantly. Her eyes rove coolly around the crowded room. Evidently she sees nothing which pleases her, no paragon worthy of her closer attention.

"I've got some excellent Buddha tucked away," Fletcher tells her. He changes tack after a silent interval. (No, not silent, Davy thinks. The room is rowdy with music, conversation, greetings. It just *seemed* silent.) "Davy's the genius in charge of the notorious Plastic Environment Project."

"Indeed?" Maggie is unenthusiastic. She moves away in the direction of the kitchen. Fletcher stares after her with transparent lust.

Angry, Davy goes the other way. He stumbles between dancers and conversationalists, finds the stagnant lee of the party where gloomy figures squat next to the enormous bookshelf and pretend engrossment in a variety of intellectual delights. Davy has no stomach for such subterfuge. Stepping on fingers, he staggers along the wall until he reaches an open French window. Beyond is the hot, dark, eucalyptus-rich garden. The air is volatile, the trees seem ripe for spontaneous combustion. He leans his forehead against the jamb and sighs.

What am I doing here? he asks himself. What am I doing anywhere? Voices babble behind him, someone sings loudly and badly; peaks of meaningless noise pierce his brain. He is afflicted ludicrously: an urgent erection, and a rush of misery so desolating that the thought of suicide touches his belly. Wiring diagrams flicker against the night sky. The elegance of his work leaves him empty. What's the point of all the bloody lights, the cunning plastic forms and extrusions, the distant cruel games he plays with his audience, the participants in his fine new art? He has *made* something, but where is the joy of it? Does he love anything? Does he love himself? Ah, Lao-Tse, where is the Tao? *I alone am confused / confused / desolate / Oh, like the sea / adrift / Oh, with no harbour / to anchor in . . .*

Davy's brow, his face, is cold and damp. He wishes for a breeze from that sullen darkness. But there is relief in despair. He utters a little involuntary sound, a broken breath drawn back, the air dry in his mouth, steps back into the room with his empty glass and collides with Marguerite Roche. Automatically he clutches Maggie's firm arm to save her from falling

"I'm terribly sorry," he blurts. "Uh—I seem to have spilled your claret. Can I get you another?"

She considers him steadily. "Thank you. David, isn't it?"

"Davy," he says. "I won't be a moment."

When he returns, she's gazing with infinite detachment into the motionless garden. Her hair is glossy and neat.

THE JUDAS MANDALA

Remarkable bones lend her rather ordinary face a touch of beauty, but the flesh about her somber eyes is already puckered with the lines of encroaching age. Excitement surges in him as he touches her elbow. "It's rather raw, I'm afraid," he tells her. "All the good stuff's gone, or the greedy bastards're hoarding it."

The woman takes the glass without a word, lifts it to her mouth for a token sip. Davy is aware of nothing but violet shadow skimming her face as a suspended lamp swings back and forth on the room's far side; the clean perfume of her skin and hair, the puzzling ambiguity of her eyes. There is no release from this moment. Numb, halting, denying the internal traitor, words come to his mouth, "Look, Maggie, there's no one else you want to see here, is there? Why don't you let me show you through the Environment? At least it's cool in there," he finishes lamely.

She appraises him in the half dark. "Why not?"

The terror, in decision, is redoubled. Maneuvers scurry in his brain. Is there anyone here with a car he can borrow? Not a chance, he decides. Bugger that, anyway. He won't be dragged back here simply to deliver someone's vehicle. We'll walk, he tells himself. It's not that far.

Somehow he keeps his cool, finds himself following Maggie through the drunken congregation of artists and fine minds. "I've got my car outside," she tells him briskly, producing the keys. She does not hand them to him.

Davy trails her along the hall, somewhat agape. Matters are moving too fast; he is not at all sure he likes the way she's taking control. And he knows that this too is an evasion, that control is predicated in knowledge, that his knowledge is a passion of wires and charges and shaped objects, that there is no intimacy in it. What the hell, he tells himself—at least she's giving me no time for cold feet. The door closes behind them and he is standing in the hot heavy night with her.

Maggie glances at him as he opens the gate for her. "This will have to be quick, Davy. I'm leaving town tomorrow and I still have some packing to do."

"Okay," he says without joy; he prepares himself, as always, for devastation and loss. "There won't be anyone in the Environment at this hour—we can go straight through without any hassles."

THE JUDAS MANDALA

The car is a tiny Blue Honda. A discreet sticker marks it as a hire-car, curiously enough. What does he know about this woman? She slides without a word into the driver's seat, reaches across and opens the passenger door for Davy. He climbs in, staring at her legs, heart thudding. Wondering what to do with his hands, he settles stiffly back in the seat. Reluctantly, he puts them in his lap. "You know the address?"

"I've seen it from the outside. It'd be difficult to miss."

"That's the idea." The Plastic Environment is on the edge of the uptown disaster area, amid decaying residential terraces and faded, blighted small businesses, in a misshapen building which came cheap because it's useless for any realistic human purpose. A fashionable discothèque, *Lot's Wife,* had been there for several months, before the city fathers closed it down to safeguard adolescent morals. It is conceivable that the patronage of the University's Fine Arts Department will suffice to save the Plastic Environment from the same wholesome fate.

The woman's driving, Davy observes, is more than competent, a satisfying mixture of sanity and verve. They park across the street from the center, sit staring for a moment at the electroluminescents writhing in arcane patterns up and down the front of the building. Davy neglects his panic and looks with pride upon his work.

The facade is festooned with loops and sheets and bubbles of plastic extrusion, glowing and shifting with startling light. Pulsing coils of mauve and green, dripping globes of crimson brilliance, flickering ultraviolets and white could be the interior of some living creature, a radioactive whale, perhaps, exposed to the hot air. A little way up the road a drunk stares at it and stares again, then lurches to vomit. Several cars slow as they pass, but there is little traffic down this sullen street. The locals are watching television; they have seen the display once.

"It's ingenious," Maggie says, getting out of the car, "but is it art?"

"It's life," Davy says. Does he believe that? Does he even think he believes it? He stands on the footpath and watches a cerise sperm chase a blushing pink ovum through recesses of darkness. Crass, he thinks suddenly. Not funny. But he says, "The twentieth century in schema." He recognizes his pomposity, knows he should have smiled, or groaned, at her jab; despite this, he continues woodenly, "I don't know if it's art. Is life art? No, of course not. Not yet. But I think life must *become* art, or we'll turn into an administered swarm of sedated robots."

They cross the street together, not touching. Davy thrusts a magnetized plastic card into a slot; the spherical, flower-petaled entrance irises, and lights come on within the center. Davy smiles in delight. The woman has audibly caught her breath as the door dilated. It *is* impressive—a technical trick, but one he's quite pleased with.

"Come into my parlor," he says, and then is desperate for words not clichés. Her presence overwhelms him: her unorthodox, compelling sexuality. Maggie's eyes rove across the constellation of tubes and loops bent surreally throughout the room. She steps in after him, making no comment.

"Just come round the side here, Maggie," he says, thankful for the demands of expertise, pushing his way past a spaghetti clump of blue pipes erupting down from the ceiling. "Won't be a moment—have to power up some of these things."

She shows no interest in the gleaming bank of switches when he enters the office. Quickly Davy activates the major Environment situations and comes out to stand beside her. More lights flicker on now, a spectrum of visual shocks. The ceiling is bathed in gliding white-on-gold curves. In the center of the room vast plastic pipes and tunnels begin slowly to pulse, swelling and subsiding like lungs, arteries, hues cycling from somber duns and grays to vivid emeralds and reds.

"A novel arrangement," Maggie says. Her poise remains sublime. If anything, she looks a trifle bored. Davy learns that his jaw is set tight; conscious effort is required to relax without tremoring. "It takes a while to warm up," he says. "Come on, we'll go into it."

A curious penetrating hum is rising in the room, baffling their ears as whirling light confuses their eyes. Gradually the hum changes into a mathematically modulated electronic score, counterpointed by the almost actinic trills and runs of a sitar.

Plastic bubbles press against their bodies as Davy leads the woman in a slow spiral toward the center of the Environment; the plastic is fleshy, yielding, then unexpectedly resilient, jabbing shoulders and hips, then feather light, translucent as soap bubbles. Suddenly Maggie laughs out loud. Davy knows pleasure so abrupt that his eyes sting: she has picked up the almost inaudible intrusion of Percy Faith and his orchestra.

"Close your eyes," Davy suggests. "Move your face and your hands about, get the textures and shapes through your skin. Play with the forms. Turn your skepticism off for a minute and let the Environment interact with your body chemistry." One of the blowers in the floor sends up a gust of biting scent, makes them both gasp. At once the artificial breeze shifts, blows a moist aroma of green things thriving in dense loam, a warm hint of freshly baked bread.

"Clever," Maggie says, gliding slowly through the great soft shapes. "In fact, it's delightful, in its own peculiar way. But it's too contrived, too ... self-conscious."

"Goddamn it, stop analyzing," he says, and sees at once no less than three levels of his anger. Only when he's alone here does the armor of his muscles soften. No doubt some deep suffocating deliberation has built this place for him so that he might come here with a woman, to touch her with the articulated product of his hands, to speak to her in a revelation removed to a safe ambiguity, to touch her ... "Let yourself react spontaneously," he says in anger. His teeth hurt as he presses them together, a hard line from the hinge of his jaw to the base of his neck. Tension jerks his belly. They move into the shimmering Environment.

Bright stars reel past sunbursts tasting of gems. Light ebbs in sluggish waves, rolling in pale bands and bands of darkness, making sea images of fronds and darting shapes. The odors are pungent, salty. Points of glare erupt in the encroaching gloom. A drumming syncopation rises and falls behind the complexities of sound, climbing, pounding through bone and nerve as glimmer makes vast shadows of the plastic shapes they drift amongst, grows and thrums and dominates their rhythms like a primordial heartbeat, the beat of the mother, the throb of the ocean, the measured pulse of two bodies coming slowly to a governed climax. ...

She's part of the rhythm now. Her limbs move freely as she forges through spheres and cylinders, streamers and shafts of light. Her eyes are closed, her mouth moist and parted. Davy watches her as he moves with her to the hidden center of the Environment, his own mouth drying in panic, watching the bounding plastic shapes touch her and the music's beat compel her steps, her breath.

And they stand before the entrance of the great tube which leads to the heart of the Environment.

He can say nothing. Go on, fool. How can she be offended? She may refuse—okay, so we go back to the foyer for a cup of coffee, and go away. But the logic of the place is lost to him, stolen by the panic. Christ, he thinks, appallingly conscious of himself standing stupidly silent at the mouth of the Tube. Say something. Say anything. Maggie opens her eyes then, blinking in the emerald light, and begins to take off her blouse.

Davy coughs convulsively. He looks away; words tumble. "Uh, you know about going through the Tube naked, then? You don't, I mean if you'd rather I—"

She holds out her blouse to him. "Where do we put our clothes, David? I assume you've built some ingenious mechanism to save us dropping our gear on the floor." She has not been wearing a bra; he wants to look at her breasts, and cannot. Wordlessly he takes the garment and places it in the hopper almost hidden beside the entrance to the Tube. Participants normally have all this spelled out in advance; even so, he notes distantly, it's a design flaw, clarity of function sacrificed to an ideal sleekness. He presses the button marked FEMALE and hands her the key to her locker module, with its chain and numbered tag.

"Oh, I see." Maggie places the chain around her neck. She opens a zipper and removes her skirt, then slips out of her panties. Her backside sags slightly. He has never seen a woman's pubic hair before. "Of course I knew about the general idea," she adds. "They made quite a point of it on *This Day Tonight*."

"We, uh, usually arrange it so people go through at intervals of about a minute," Davy blurts. "The law . . ." He realizes he's still standing fully clothed and wrenches at his T-shirt. "I imagine so," Maggie says dryly. She steps into ultramarine shadow, pushes her hand into the warm cleft of the Tube, vanishes into it.

Davy rips at his clothes, his erection monstrous, hurls the clothes helter-skelter into the next module and seizes the key. His sweat is acrid through the mixed scents and fragrances of the Environment. A cool breeze touches his bare legs. He plunges into the Tube.

Plastic surfaces, slick and alien, press his body. He has been through the Tube thirty times, and each time it makes the hair rise on his skin. He knows a brief claustrophobic horror; then it is gone, vanquished by amazement and delight at the fluid runs of light rippling the interior of the walls, the extraordinary sensation of sliding and gliding in the slipstream of time.

The Tube curves like a snake, like an intestine, like—of course—a vagina. Davy slithers in pursuit of the naked woman and fails to catch a glimpse of her. He is feverish. The Tube buckles and glistens. He slides and wriggles through it. He falls into thick, sweet grass.

A soft hand catches Davy's bare thigh. Maggie giggles like a child of ten, rolls past him in the gentle light and tugs at tufts of grass. She buries her face in it, snapping her teeth, and laughs again. He looks in bewilderment and is infected, to his distant astonishment, with her mirth. They roll about in the grass, and his sexual pressures are subsumed in some larger expansion; playful as puppies, touching by accident and design, they give themselves to the moment. When he reaches for her it is without prompting, without caution, and she waits for him.

He explores her, and marvels. His mouth and his hands and his chest and his limbs find her breasts and her thighs and all the wet and dry and soft and hard places of her body. When he fumbles she moves to meet him; when he dare not spend himself quickly she shows him her ears and her throat and her arms and the bones of her back and saves him; when, incredibly, she quakes and cries out and bites his arm in the time of her reward he shouts for her pleasure, and moments later groans to his own. And he marvels again at her leanness and her swollen mouth, at the slow ebbing tides of languor that rock them both almost to sleep. The grass abrades his back; her breast is soft against his side; his fingers touch her lips in quiet contentment.

Maggie sits up, then, and shakes her hair.

"This is the clever part, Davy," she says. "The grass garden in the heart of the plastic universe."

"An important part," he says. "But the rest is important, too. It's all the world—you can't chop it apart and take

THE JUDAS MANDALA

the bits you want." He sends his fingers along the smooth curve of her back, along her arm; they bobble over an inoculation scar. "I am you and you are me." He smiles up at her.

In an epiphany of astounding contact, she turns her head and looks at him. "That's what you have to find out, David," she says. Then she takes herself away, dizzyingly, like an optical illusion, without moving her eyes; and she climbs to her feet and glances around the enclosure. "I've got that packing to do."

He is, in that instant, desolated. He is incredulous. "Jesus, are you in that much of a hurry?"

Something close to anguish comes and goes in her face. He sees it merely as annoyance. She goes to the exit. "I'll drop you off at your house. Is there a shower here?"

Davy rises, follows her out. "Yes, pet. And your clothes, just over there in the women's dressing room. Look—"

"Be as quick as you can, Davy."

"All right." He goes into the men's dressing room, stands beside the shower until hot water replaces cold. Hard burning needles strike his tingling flesh. He turns his face into the hot rush of water and seeks to retain his joy. "Don't be bloody ridiculous," he says out loud, and water runs into his mouth. He splutters, and angrily turns off the taps. Think of it in the abstract, he tells himself. Not Maggie Roche. An instrument of initiation. The traitor advises him desperately. He is alarmed and chilled. Her image invades him. He grabs a towel and rubs furiously.

She's waiting for him in the lobby when he comes out, his beard still wet.

"Davy, I really am in a hell of a hurry."

He cannot believe what is happening. "Yeah. I'll just turn the Environment off." In the office he switches out the lights, the blowers, even the exterior facade: the numerous electronic and mechanical systems which constitute his armor and his nerves. Others have built it for him, but the design, the conception is his. It is, he realizes at some deep level, a clone: his vision of his own DNA externalized. If it has betrayed him, it is because he has betrayed himself.

Davy walks back to her, his boots echoing mournfully on the hard floor. She is glancing at her watch. Something burns in him like acid, like improbably potent emotion rebounding from blankness and consuming itself.

"It was good of you to show me," Maggie says. The trick door cycles closed behind them. Hot, humid night assaults their cool skin.

"My pleasure," Davy says, with distant rage. Maggie opens the passenger door of the little Honda and he climbs in beside her. "Look," he says abruptly, "when will you be back from Perth?"

She slides in the ignition key, starts the motor. "I'll be very busy," she says remotely. "I don't think there'll be any point in your calling me. If you'll tell me your address, I'll drop you off home."

His hand jumps of its own will, pulls out the ignition key. "Christ, Maggie, what do you—"

Her face is rigid, and for a moment he thinks she's going to strike him. Instead she holds out her hand for the key. "Stop acting like a child," she says. "I'm tired, and I'm very rapidly becoming bored."

He is in a panic of dread and self-doubt. Everything is receding; sounds come faintly and distorted. He seizes the closest explanation, knows it for melodrama, but turns his pain upon her in bafflement and spite. "You incredible bitch." In this extremity, this unreality, he finds a bizarre courage. "It's a game you play, is it? How am I performing, Maggie? Is it satis—"

She does hit him then. The blow sends his head cracking against the metal door frame. "Get out," she says. "Give me the keys and get out."

Davy starts to laugh. He opens his door, throws the keys at her feet. She leans forward against the wheel. "You poor frigid cow," he says, staring at her through the open door. "You'll never know how much you gave me." He slams the door, then, and walks back across the street. Behind him, as he enters the Plastic Environment, he hears the car roar into life. He refuses to turn his head as the wheels spin with a screech of rubber.

The lights come on inside the Environment. Davy Elfield stands for a moment gazing at the spirals and twists of polymer extrusion. He recognizes dimly that something terrible has been wrought in him, that he is changed, changed utterly, in the twinkling of an eye. Memories of her body ricochet from every glowing plastic surface. It is not her body which has wounded him, but he knows that he is wounded. His shoulders slump, and the anger and grief begin their rage through him, and with systematic ferocity Davy starts to tear the place to pieces.

In the midst of his single-minded fury he hears a footfall behind him, a muffled cry.

First anger: "What the hell are you doing here?" She is hardly older than himself, extraordinarily beautiful.

Then shame: "Who are you?" he shouts, aghast at the self-revelation he sees on every side of him. "My God, you haven't been lurking in here all along, have you?" He needs an outlet; his embarrassment could recoil, twist, vomit into rage at her intrusion. Yet the turmoil in his soul is more profound than that, he knows that he is not going to turn on this woman like a beast. He presses an arm against his laboring chest.

"My name is Sriyanie N'Zanvy," the lovely white-haired woman tells him.

History shudders.

Sydney 1967—New York 1981

From the finest writers of science fiction and fantasy now comes the excitement of

"science fantasy."

Read some of today's best science fantasy, now available from Pocket Books.

FLOATING WORLDS
by Cecelia Holland — 83147/$2.95

E PLURIBUS UNICORN
by Theodore Sturgeon — 83149/$1.95

THE DYING EARTH
by Jack Vance — 44184/$2.25

THE GREAT FETISH
by L. Sprague de Camp — 83161/$1.95

EYES OF THE OVERWORLD
by Jack Vance — 83292/$1.95

THE BLESSING PAPERS
by William Barnwell — 83219/$2.50

THE DEVIL'S GAME
by Poul Anderson — 83689/$2.50

POCKET BOOKS Department SFF
1230 Avenue of the Americas, New York, N.Y. 10020

Please send me the books I have checked above. I am enclosing $_____ (please add 50¢ to cover postage and handling for each order, N.Y.S. and N.Y.C. residents please add appropriate sales tax). Send check or money order—no cash or C.O.D.s please. Allow up to six weeks for delivery.

NAME_____

ADDRESS_____

CITY_____ STATE/ZIP_____

The long-awaited new adventure by the greatest writing team in science fiction—

OVER 3 MILLION OF THEIR BOOKS IN PRINT!

LARRY NIVEN and JERRY POURNELLE!

OATH of FEALTY

A gripping epic of a near-future America, of a high-technology Utopia rising above the ruins of Los Angeles—and its desperate struggle to survive the awesome forces that surround it!

The authors of **The Mote in God's Eye, Inferno** and **Lucifer's Hammer** surpass the excitement and suspense of their earlier books in a novel that will leave you breathless!

POCKET BOOKS

472

ON THE OTHER SIDE OF TIME AND SPACE

Stories of Fantastic, Futuristic Worlds That Illuminate Universes

Pocket Books offers the best in Science Fiction — a genre whose time has come.

____ 43684	JUNIPER TIME	
	Kate Wilhelm	$2.75
____ 41593	RUINS OF ISIS	
	Marion Zimmer Bradley	$2.25
____ 82917	ROAD TO CORLAY	
	Richard Cowper	$1.95
____ 82876	A WORLD BETWEEN	
	Norman Spinrad	$2.25
____ 81207	JOURNEY	
	Marta Randall	$1.95
____ 42882	COLONY	
	Ben Bova	$2.95
____ 82835	EYES OF FIRE	
	Michael Bishop	$2.25
____ 43288	THE DEMU TRILOGY	
	F. M. Busby	$3.50
____ 81130	DYING OF THE LIGHT	
	George R. R. Martin	$1.95

POCKET BOOKS, Department SFT
1230 Avenue of the Americas, New York, N.Y. 10020

Please send me the books I have checked above. I am enclosing $_____ (please add 50¢ to cover postage and handling for each order, N.Y.S. and N.Y.C. residents please add appropriate sales tax). Send check or money order—no cash or C.O.D.s please. Allow up to six weeks for delivery.

NAME_____

ADDRESS_____

CITY_____ STATE/ZIP_____